Ricardo Piglia is Professor of Latin American Literature at Princeton University and is the author, among other works, of Respiración artificial (1980) La ciudad ausente (1992) and Crítica y ficción (1986) – a collection of interviews and essays on key Argentine writers such as Borges, Arlt and Sarmiento.

Amanda Hopkinson is a Senior Research Fellow at Cardiff University. Her previous translations include José Saramago's Voyage to Portugal and Paul Coelho's The Devil and Miss Prym.

# Money to Burn

## Ricardo Piglia

*Translated by*
*Amanda Hopkinson*

**Granta Books**
London · New York

Granta Publications, 2/3 Hanover Yard, Noel Road, London N1 8BE

First published in Great Britain by Granta Books 2003

A CIP catalogue record for this book
is available from the British Library.

1 3 5 7 9 10 8 6 4 2

Typeset by M Rules
Printed and bound by
Legoprint, Italy

*To Gerardo Gandini*

*'After all, what is robbing a bank compared to founding one?'*

BERTOLT BRECHT

# Money
# to Burn

# I

They are called the twins because they're inseparable. But they aren't brothers, nor do they even look like one another. In fact, it would be hard to find two more different physical types. What they have in common is a way of looking at you, with their pale, placid eyes, a savage stare in a suspicious face. Dorda is heavy, quiet, with a ruddy face and an easy smile. Brignone is thin, slightly built, agile, has black hair and a complexion so pallid, it looks as if he's spent more time in jail than he actually has. *understatement => matter of fact*

They got off the subway at Bulnes station and paused before the window of a photography shop to check they weren't being followed. They were bound to attract attention with their extravagant looks, like a couple of boxers, or undertakers escaped from a funeral parlour. They were elegantly and carefully dressed in black double-breasted suits, with cropped hair and manicured nails. The evening was calm, one of those clear, late spring afternoons with a white, translucent light. People were just leaving their offices to return home, an air of utter absorption about them.

They waited for the traffic lights to change and crossed Santa Fe Avenue, leading towards Arenales Street. They'd boarded the subway at Constitución and made a number of changes, making sure that nobody was following them. Dorda was very superstitious, forever spotting negative signals, and engaged in numerous secret rituals, which tended to complicate his life. He liked riding the subways, moving beneath the yellow light of platforms and tunnels, getting into carriages and letting himself be carried along. Whenever he was in danger (and he was always in danger) he felt secure and protected travelling through the city's entrails like that. It was simple, really, to escape detection by the undercover cops. All that was required was for him to nip back on to the empty platform at the last possible moment, allowing the train to go on without him, in order to confirm that he was in the clear.

Brignone was trying to calm him down.

'It'll turn out right, everything's under control.'

'I don't like there being so many people mixed up in it.'

'If something's going to happen to you, it'll happen whether anyone else is mixed up in it or not. If you catch a dose of bad luck, there's nobody can save you. If you stopped to buy cigarettes, you could be off and lost forever in just a minute.'

'And why do we all have to meet up now?'

An initial raid has to be properly planned, after which it's essential to move fast to prevent word getting out. Fast means two or three days, from when you get the first information until the time you finally go to ground in a neighbouring country. You always have to pay, laying out money up front, while juggling with the risk that whoever sells you the information might also be selling it elsewhere.

The twins set off to their post on a block along Arenales Street. A clean position in a safe quarter of town, on the alley leading to the beer factory. They had rented it as an operational centre from which to coordinate all their movements.

'It's a bachelor pad in a swanky district, like a safehouse where you can set things up and hang out,' Malito had told them, when he contracted them in.

The twins were heavyweights, men of action, and Malito had come down in their favour, putting them in charge of information-gathering. At the same time, Malito remained mistrustful, that was for sure, guarding the loot with every possible security measure, each one under his control, an invalid who never let himself be seen. He was the invisible man, the magical brain, operating at a distance, with his own strange set of circuits and contacts and connections, 'Mad Mala', as mad Dorda called him. Because he was anyway called Malito, that was his real surname. Back in Devoto he'd known a cop called Hangman, which must have been even worse. To be called Hangman, or Slave, or even, like another of their acquaintances, Traitor – with surnames like that around, better to be called Malito. The rest of them had nicknames (Brignone was the Kid, Dorda was the Blond Gaucho) but Malito was his own nickname. Ratfaced, his eyes clinging either side of his nose, chinless, utterly serene, with his dyed hair and a woman's hands, a phenomenal intelligence. He knew about motors, circuits, could assemble a bomb in minutes, fiddling with his fingers just so, adjusting the timer, the little flasks of nitrate, all without looking. The hands of a blind man or a pianist, with the capacity to send a whole police station up in smoke.

Malito was the boss and had made his plans and prepared his contacts with politicians and the police who furnished him with data, maps, details and to whom, in return, he would give half of the proceeds. There were a whole lot of players in this game, but Malito was convinced he had at least ten to twelve hours' advantage over the others, that he could leave them waiting for their pay-off and escape with the dough, across the border into Uruguay.

That afternoon they'd split themselves into two groups. The twins were off to the Arenales apartment to carefully review every step of the operation once again. Meanwhile Malito rented a room in the hotel opposite the place where they were planning to mount the assault. From the hotel window he could see San Fernando Square and the Provincial Bank building. He tried to visualize their movements, the split-second timing of the raid, the getaway against the one-way traffic and the density of the flow of cars at that hour.

The pick-up truck belonging to the treasurer would leave to the left, advancing clockwise, obliged to approach from the front and halt before entering the gateway of the Town Hall. The one-way system made it necessary for it to circle the entire square and cut them off in midstream. They had to kill the driver and all the guards before they could draw their weapons, since the only thing going for them was the element of surprise.

Some witnesses swore they'd seen Malito in the hotel with a woman. Others swore they'd only seen two guys and definitely no woman. One of the pair was a skinny and nervous youth, constantly injecting himself, Twisty Bazán, who, that afternoon, really was in the San Fernando hotel room with Malito, observing every movement at the Bank from the window overlooking the street. Following the robbery, the police cleared out the place and in the bathroom they found syringes, a lighter and the remaining crystals. The police assumed that Twisty was the young man who'd gone down to the bar and asked for an alcohol warmer. As usual, the witnesses all contradict one another, but they all agree that the youth resembled an actor and that he had a wild look about him. From this it was inferred that it was he who'd been injecting heroin just before the robbery and that he'd requested the lighter in order to heat the drug. From then on the witnesses began calling him 'the Lad'. And thereafter confusion reigned in distinguishing between Bazán and Brignone, as several witnesses were certain that the two of them were one whom everyone called the Lad. A highly nervous skinny young guy, who held his gun in his left hand, with its barrel pointed skywards, as though he were a plain-clothes cop. Eye-witnesses in situations like these can sense their blood racing with adrenaline, causing them to become emotional and then clouded because they have witnessed an event simultaneously clear and confusing to them. Some averred they had seen a car crossing just in front of the pick-up and heard a racket, with one guy on the ground kicking his feet as he died.

Perhaps they'd thought of taking refuge in the hotel following the robbery, in case they didn't manage to get away.

What was most likely was that they had two guys covering the Bank from the hotel and three more who arrived in a Chevrolet 400 'well fitted out' according to every version. Fast as a bullet, that car. Perhaps one of the criminals was a mechanic responsible for fine-tuning the engine at over 5,000 revs, converting it into a sedan as smooth as silk.

San Fernando is a residential suburb of Buenos Aires, its peaceful leafy streets lined with grand private mansions from the early years of the twentieth century, now either transformed into schools or abandoned on the heights above the river.

The square was tranquil in the white light of spring.

While Malito and Twisty Bazán spent the afternoon and evening in the San Fernando hotel, the rest of the gang shut themselves into the flat on Arenales Street. They had heisted a car out in the province and stored it in the basement garage, then unloaded the gear and the weapons up through the service stairway and stayed inside, with the blinds pulled down, to await their orders.

There could be nothing worse than the evening before, with everything lined up ready to go out on the streets and start shooting, each of them believing himself clairvoyant, capable of seeing visions, any old thing appearing as a sign of ill omen, or an informer looking for unusual signs of movement and passing info on to the police who then go and set an ambush to greet your arrival, because if your luck's down, or so Dorda says, you have to call the whole thing off, return to point zero, and leave well alone for another month before trying again.

The handover was on the twenty-eighth of every month, at three in the afternoon: the loot was moved from the

Provincial Bank to the Town Council offices. A wagonload of cash, close on 600,000 dollars, trundling around the block, following the lines of the square from left to right, a total of seven minutes from when the money appeared in the doorway of the Bank to getting it loaded on to the station wagon and from there inside the Town Council, by the back door. ~~'I'll tell you one thing, little bro,~~ Dorda smiled at the Kid Brignone, 'you've never been mixed up in anything half as "scientific" as this, we've got the lot under control.'

The Kid stared at him uncertainly, drinking beer from the neck of the bottle, stretched out on the sofa, shoeless and in his shirtsleeves, facing the shimmering and soundless television set in the living-room that looked out over Arenales Street. The flat was new, clean, and silent, all its papers in order. The gang's driver, 'Crow' Mereles, had rented it for his 'girlfriend', as he called her, and everyone in the district had been given to assume that Mereles was a landowner from Buenos Aires province who supported the Girl and her family. Right now the girlfriend's family had gone on holiday to Mar del Plata and the flat had been converted into what Malito called his operational base.

That night they had to go carefully, without letting themselves be spotted, without talking to anyone, lying low. Downstairs there was a telephone, in the building's lower basement, and from there it was possible to call through to the room in the San Fernando hotel every two or three hours. As Malito told them: 'Always use the phone in the garage, never ring out from the house phone.'

He had a number of obsessions, this Malito: the phone was one of them. According to him, every phone in the city was tapped. But he also had other manias, Mad Mala did, according to Dorda the Loopy. He couldn't stand sunlight, couldn't stand seeing lots of people together, and was continually wiping down his hands with pure alcohol. He liked the dry refreshing sensation of the alcohol on his skin. His father had been a doctor and he would say that doctors always wash their hands in alcohol, right up to the elbows, after finishing their consultations, so he inherited the habit from him.

'Every germ,' Malito loved to explain, 'gets transmitted through the hands, via the fingernails. If people refrained from shaking hands, at least ten per cent of the population wouldn't die, those who now die from all the hand bugs.'

Those who die through violence (according to him) are less than half the number of those dead of infectious diseases and nobody takes the doctors into custody (Malito laughed out loud at his joke). Sometimes he liked to imagine the women and children he passed in the street wearing surgeons' rubber gloves and hygienic masks, every citizen of the capital in a mask, to avert contact and avoid contagion.

Malito was from Rosario and had taken his degree course in Engineering up to the fourth year. At times he got them to call him the Engineer, although in secret they all called him Stripey. That was because a further reason for his madness was the marks all over his body, still showing as thick weals, a legacy of being whipped at a police station in Turdera with metal springs stripped from a bed by the brute of a provincial policeman. Malito later went after him, and seized him late one night when the guy was just getting out of a bus, and drowned him in a puddle. He forced him to his knees, plunged his face in the mud, and it's said he pulled down his trousers and raped him while the cop struggled to try to free himself with his head under water. Or so it's said, one never knows. Nice type, that Malito, pushy, a bit on the sly side. Not many like him in these parts. He always managed to get others to do what he wanted, as if it were all their own idea. On the other hand, nobody had ever encountered a more fortunate fellow than Malito. He possessed a god of his own to watch over him. And a halo of perfection which led to everyone wanting to work with him. That was why in the space of two days he had organized the assault on the wages van of the San Fernando municipality. No minor matter, or no small beer (according to Twisty Bazán), with at least a half-million in play.

So there was the phone in a wooden box, downstairs in the garage to the flat on Arenales Street, from which they talked to Malito the previous night.

Malito envisaged the robbery as a military operation and had issued them all with strict instructions, so the plotters now wanted to go over the entire plan one last time.

Crow Mereles, a thin guy with bulging eyes, had a sheet of paper showing a plan of the square and was finishing off drawing in the final details.

'We have four minutes. The van is coming from the Bank and has to go this way around the square. Am I right or am I right?'

The guy handing it over was a tango singer who called himself Fontán Reyes; he'd been the last to arrive at the flat on Arenales Street, looked pale and nervous, and sat himself down in a corner. Following the Crow's question, everyone remained silent and stared in his direction. Eventually Reyes got up and went over to the table.

'The van arrives with its windows open,' he said.

Everything had to be done in broad daylight, at ten past

three in the afternoon, and in the town centre of San Fernando. The wages money was taken out of the Bank and transported to the Town Hall, only 200 metres away. Given the one-way system, the wages van had to follow the direction of the traffic all the way around the square.

'It takes on average between seven and ten minutes, depending on the traffic.'

'And how many guards accompany it?'

'Two policemen, here and here. With the guy in the van, that makes three.'

Reyes is nervous. Scared to death, if the truth were told (as he was later to admit). Fontán Reyes is his *nom d'artiste*. His real name is Atir Omar Nocito and he's thirty-nine years old, and he used to sing with Juan Sánchez Gorio's orchestra and he'd acted on radio and television, and he'd even managed to record a double-sided tango record with 'Esta noche de copas' and 'Noche de locura', accompanied on the piano by Osvaldo Manzi. His moment of glory came with the Carnival in 1960, when he made his debut with Héctor Varela as Argentino Ledesma's heir apparent. Then he began to have drug problems. In June he went to Chile to duet with Raúl Lavié, but within a month he'd lost his voice and couldn't speak. Too much cocaine, everyone assumed. What's for sure is that he was obliged to return home and thus began his run of lousy luck, so he ended up singing in a bar in Almagro, to guitar accompaniment. Recently he'd managed a few slots at festivals, dances at local clubs, sporadically touring the low-life dives in outer Buenos Aires.

Luck is a strange commodity and chooses to turn up when least expected. One night, in a rundown tavern, some guys were out looking for Reyes to offer him a gig and, as if in a dream, he learnt of a major cash delivery, and realized he was in a position to go for the big time, and he gambled everything on one throw of the dice. He called Malito. Fontán Reyes wanted to get in and then out sharpish, but that afternoon in the flat on Arenales Street he found himself getting thoroughly boxed in, he didn't know which way to turn, he was pathetically afraid, this down-at-heel tango singer, afraid of everything (especially, he said, of Gaucho Dorda, a headcase, a mental subnormal), of being killed before they gave him his share, of being handed over, of being used as a dupe by the police. He was desperate, down and out, wanting to cut loose. His dream was to give it his best shot, to get paid and take off, start all over again in another place (changing his name, changing his country), imagining that with the money he could open an Argentinian restaurant in New York, entertaining a *latino* clientele. On one occasion he'd stopped off in Manhattan with Juan Sánchez Gorio and spent a wild night at Charlie's on West 53rd Street, a restaurant managed by a Cuban crazy about tango. He needed the dough to invest, because the Cuban had promised to help him if he arrived in New York with 'start-up capital', but everything got more dangerous by the day since he'd thrown in his lot with these guys who seemed to be forever hallucinating, as though they were perpetually high. They laughed at anything and everything and never went to sleep. Hard-boiled characters, assassins who enjoyed killing for its own sake, not exactly the kind of people one could trust.

His uncle, Nino Nocito, was an avid Peronist supporter, elected to represent the wealthy Zona Norte, a leading figure in the Popular Unity party and interim president of the San Fernando Town Council. A few days earlier, the uncle had advised him of a meeting of the finance committee and he'd got the whole picture. The same evening Nocito went to hear his nephew sing in a low-life dive on Serrano and Honduras and, well away on his second bottle of wine, he began to sing himself.

'Fontán . . . there's at least five million in it.'

They needed to employ a gang of thieves of the utmost trustworthiness, a group of professionals to put in charge of the operation. Reyes had to guarantee that his uncle would be taken care of.

'Nobody can possibly know that I am mixed up in this. Nobody,' Nocito said. Nor did he, in his turn, wish to know who was going to be in on the job. He only wanted a half of a half, meaning a clean 75,000 dollars (according to his calculations).

Fontán Reyes was told to wait for them in a house on Martínez Street where they were going to go to ground immediately after the robbery. They reckoned that within a half-hour everything could be sorted.

'If we don't arrive within the half-hour,' announced Crow Mereles, 'that means we're moving on to second post.'

Fontán Reyes had no idea where the next post was, nor was he at all sure what 'second post' meant. Malito had got to know the system through Nando Heguilein, a former member of the National Liberation Alliance, with whom he had become friends when they were both prisoners in the Sierra Chica a while ago. A cellular structure prevents everything collapsing like a chain of dominoes and gives you time to get out (according to Nando). You always have to cover your retreat.

'And so?' inquired Fontán Reyes. 'What if they don't arrive?'

'And so,' answered the Blond Gaucho, 'you'd need to hide your pretty face.'

'And so that'd tell us there must be some sort of problem,' went on Mereles.

Fontán Reyes observed the loaded weapons on the table and for the first time realized that he'd played for stakes of all-or-nothing. Until then he'd worked as their cover on a few dirty deals for his friends. He'd concealed them, following a robbery, in his house at Olivos, he'd brought the dope into Montevideo and had sold on a few 'raviolis' – 'wraps' – in seedy downtown bars. Easy work, but this time was different. Arms were involved, and probably corpses, and he was a direct accomplice. Naturally, he was risking himself for a decent sum.

'At the very least,' his uncle had told him, 'it works out at a million pesos a head.'

With 100,000 dollars he could open his bar in New York. A place where he could live out his retirement in peace.

'Do you have somewhere to go tonight?' inquired Mereles, and Fontán Reyes jumped with surprise.

He was going to wait for them in a place no one else knew about, then call them up by phone.

'The operation is due to last six minutes,' insisted the Kid. 'Any longer and it gets too dangerous because there are two police points and a short-wave radio covering the whole twenty blocks.'

'The key to it all,' said Fontán Reyes, 'is that there are no deep throats.'

'Spoken like one who knows,' said Dorda.

At this moment the door opened and a young blonde woman, almost a girl, dressed in a miniskirt and a flowery blouse, came into the room. She was barefoot and embraced Mereles.

'Do you have some for me, little Daddy?' she asked.

Mereles pushed some cocaine on a mirror over towards her and the Girl moved to his side and began chopping at it with a razor. Then she warmed it with a lighter while she hummed Paul McCartney's 'Yesterday'. She took out a 50-peso note, rolled it up into a cone, inserted it into one nostril and inhaled with a gentle snort. Dorda looked on in amazement and noticed how the Girl wasn't wearing a bra, you could see her breasts through her light blouse.

'Delay, medium term, ten minutes, according to the traffic.'

'There'll be two guards and a cop,' recited Brignone.

'We have to kill the lot of them,' said Dorda suddenly. 'If you leave witnesses, they'll lock you up 'cause they're all out to do the rounds and spit on you.'

The young girl's life had suddenly changed and she went along with them in the conviction that it wasn't going to offer her another chance like this. Her name was Blanca Galeano. In January she had travelled all by herself to Mar del Plata to visit a friend and celebrate, because she'd just got through her exams in the third year of secondary school a month earlier. On the Rambla one afternoon she'd got to know Mereles, a thin guy who was staying at the Provincial Hotel. Mereles introduced himself as the son of a landowner from Buenos Aires province, and Blanquita believed him. She had just reached her fifteenth birthday and by the time she'd learnt who Crow Mereles was and what he did, she was past caring. (On the contrary, she fancied him like crazy, fired by the idea of a gangster who loaded her with presents, and who pleased and excited her more and more.)

She began living with him and the guys from the gang followed her with their eyes like starving dogs. Once on some wasteland, she had seen a cage of dogs dying of hunger, all chained up, who entwined and plaited themselves around one another, then threw themselves hungrily on whatever appeared, and these guys gave her exactly the same impression. If Mereles let them loose, they would all leap on her. Sooner or later, she knew, it was bound to happen. She imagined them staring at her if she walked by undressed, in her high heels, then saw herself in bed with the Kid, as Mereles had sometimes provoked her to. 'Do you want me to bring him here?' the degenerate would ask her and she'd begin to feel the heat. She liked that twin, pale as he was, he seemed to be about the same age as herself. But he was a faggot (according to the Crow). 'Or maybe you like the big guy?' Mereles would ask her, 'look what rough trade he is,' and Blanca would laugh and throw herself at him. 'Gimme,' she'd say, 'little Daddy.' Naked, in her high heels, the Girl strutted about, until he shoved her up against the mirror, and she leaned over the bench for him to have his way with her.

She didn't want to know what the guys were planning and returned to her room. They were plotting something heavy (because something was always being plotted when they gathered to speak in low voices and spent days without leaving the house). She needed to study because she still had to deliver two subjects to obtain enough credits to finish secondary school. She was going to spend a few months with Mereles – rather like taking a holiday – and then everything was to go back to how it was before. 'You have to make the most of being young while you can,' her mother told her when she began bringing home the money. Her father, Don

Antonio Galeano, ~~was away with the fairies~~, he knew nothing about anything, went to work in the Sanitation Department, in a building that resembled a palace, on Río Bamba and Córdoba. Then her mum was bound to come along and ruin everything, forever complaining about her father, who never earned above the minimum salary, and when she got wind of her Girl's altered circumstances she began stopping in alone with her, to get her to spill the beans. And in the end, daughters always do what their mothers want. When at last the mother came to meet Mereles, she took one look at the pervert Crow's eyes glued to her breasts and began to laugh out loud. The Girl stared at her and learnt that it was possible to be jealous of one's own mother. 'You look like sisters,' said Mereles, 'please permit me to give you a kiss.'

'Sure, honey,' said the mother, 'you have to look after Blanquita for me, 'cause beware if her father finds out . . .'

'Finds out what?'

That he was married. ~~Married and separated and always going with cheap country girls he'd picked up in cabarets down on the harbour.~~

The Girl threw herself on the bed with her maths book and began thinking of other things. Mereles had promised to take her to Brazil to see the Carnival. Voices were lowered on the other side of the door, and she couldn't hear anything until a while later some giggles wafted through to her.

Dorda tended to seem a little far gone and was attached to the notion of failure, viewing everything pessimistically yet always cracking disastrous jokes, so that ultimately everyone decided they had a good time with him.

'They're going to shut off the route out of the square and we're going to be trapped and then they'll kill us like curs.'

'Don't be an idiot, Gaucho,' said the Crow, 'Daddy will do the driving and will get you out by mounting the car on to the pavement, so avoiding all the cops.'

Dorda began laughing, the spectacle of the car setting off against the traffic, riding on the pavement, headed towards the square in the midst of bullets and corpses, amused him no end.

# 2

The day of the robbery dawned fine and clear. At 15.02 on Wednesday 27 September 1965, the bank-clerk Alberto Martínez Tobar went to work at the cash desk in the San Fernando branch of the Provincial Bank of Buenos Aires. He was a tall fellow, red-faced and bug-eyed, who had recently celebrated his fortieth birthday and who only had a few more hours to live. He cracked jokes with the girls in the accounts section, and went down to the basement where the strong-boxes were stored beside the black table stacked with the bags of money. There employees in their shirtsleeves counted notes, under the artificial light and noise of the ventilators.

An underground tomb, a jail stashed with money, the bank cashier had thought. He had lived all his life in San Fernando and his father had worked for the Town Hall before him. He had a daughter who suffered acutely with her nerves, and it was costing him a fortune to have her attended to. Many times over, he had considered the possibility of stealing the money handed over into his safekeeping on a monthly basis. He had even gone as far as to mention it to his wife.

On occasion he'd thought it'd be a simple matter to bring in a dummy briefcase, identical to the rest, filled with counterfeit money. It could be substituted for one of the others, and he could then walk out with serenity. It would only require arranging with the bank-clerk who happened to be a childhood friend. They could split the cash and carry on leading their lives as normal. The fortune would accrue to their children. He visualized the money kept in a secret safe in his cupboard, the money invested under a false number in a Swiss bank, the money hidden in a mattress, he imagined himself sleeping with the wads stored under the ticking, feeling them rustle as he tossed and turned during his nights of insomnia. On recent nights, when he couldn't sleep, he had told his wife how he contemplated effecting these changes. He spoke into the darkness and she listened to him, in silence. It was one of those ideas which kept him alive, and it added a certain spirit of adventure and a certain personal interest in the money transfers he made on a monthly basis.

This particular afternoon, he deposited the briefcases on top of the table and the colleague with his green visor looked at the payment slip with its signatures and its stamps and began separating out wads of 10,000 pesos. There was a heap of money, 7,203,960 pesos to pay staff salaries and the costs of repairing the municipal sanitation works. They put the wads of new notes into the black briefcases, the leather worn through use, stuffing even the pleats and side pockets.

Before leaving the Bank, Martínez Tobar complied with the security measures and attached the case to his left wrist with a small chain anchored with a padlock. Later on, someone was to say that he paid the ultimate price for this useless precaution.

When he went out into the street he saw nothing: nobody sees anything in the moments leading up to a robbery. A wind whips up without warning and a guy gets knocked down, perhaps with a sharp blow to the back of the head, never knowing what happened. If anyone observes something suspicious afoot, he's bound to be dismissed as a timorous sort, already traumatized by a previous experience, and who's now convinced that history is about to repeat itself.

Martínez Tobar looked at what he always noticed without scrutiny: the woman with the little fairground kiosk, the boy racing his dog, the store-keeper reopening for business after the siesta hour, but he failed to see Twisty on the lookout in the bar, propped up against the counter, knocking back a gin and studying the legs of the pregnant girl who came out of the shop next door. Pregnant women excited Twisty, and he remembered the movements of the woman in a house on Saavedra Street, while her husband was away at the office and he was still a young conscript. He had met her on the subway, when he gave up his seat to her and the woman started chatting to him, and he began enjoying her company. She was the same age as Twisty, twenty years old, her six-month pregnancy stretching her skin so taut it appeared transparent and they had to seek out the weirdest positions to be able to make it, he could only penetrate her if he propped himself up with one foot on the bed, which was when she turned her face and smiled at him. It distracted him to remember the woman in Saavedra, called either Graciela or Dora, but then he reverted to feeling tense because he saw the fellow leaving the bank with the briefcase and the money. He looked at his watch. Timed to the precise second.

The two police guards chatted on the pavement. One of the Town Hall clerks, Abraham Spector, a huge and heavy fellow, tied his shoes with difficulty, leaning up against the bumpers of the pick-up. The square was quiet, tranquil even.

'What's up, Fatso?' asked the clerk, and then greeted the security guys and got into the truck.

The guards travelled in the rear seat, guys with the faces of sleepwalkers, heavy, their weapons across their laps, ex-gendarmes, former sharpshooters, retired junior officers, forever guarding somebody else's money, somebody else's women, imported cars, great mansions, faithful hounds, in total confidence, always armed and in heavy boots. One of them was called Juan José Balacco, he was sixty years old and a former police commissioner, and the other was a legal cop from the San Fernando first division, an eighteen-year-old heavyweight, Francisco Otero, whom everyone called Ringo Bonavena, because he wanted to be a boxer and trained every night in the Excursionistas gym with a Japanese trainer who had promised to make him champion of Argentina.

They had to go back across the 200 metres that separated the Bank (on one corner of the square) from the Town Hall (on the other corner).

'We're a little late,' Spector said.

The clerk set the engine running. The pick-up proceeded

along Third of February Street at walking pace and when it turned the corner there was a screech of rubber on tarmac and the sound of another car accelerating alongside them.

The car was on top of them, driving against the one-way system, shooting through, as though driverless, and screeched to a halt.

'What does this madman think he's doing?' asked Martínez Tobar, still prepared to be amused.

Two guys leapt on to the pavement and one pulled a woman's stocking over his face (or so some witnesses said). He held a pair of scissors and stretched the nylon with the tips of his fingers, then, the stocking already pulled over his head, he slashed two holes level with his eyes.

Spector was a large man, with a look of helplessness about him, wearing a striped shirt blotched with sweat. Of the four of them travelling in the pick-up, he was the only one to survive. He threw himself on the floor and they fired at him from above, but they hit the metal lid of his pocket watch, which deflected the bullet. A miracle (that he happened to be wearing his father's pocket watch). He was sitting on the pavement outside the Bank, suffocating, watching people hurry by and the ambulances pass. Journalists were gathering at the spot and the police cordoned off the street. Eventually a patrol car halted and Police Commissioner Silva stepped down. He was the chief of police for the Zona Norte of Greater Buenos Aires and in charge of the operation. He got down from his car, dressed in plain clothes, with a pistol cocked in his left hand and a walkie-talkie in his right, out of which you could hear voices giving orders and dictating numbers, and he approached Spector.

'Come with me,' he said.

Following a moment's uncertainty, Spector got up, slow and scared, and followed him.

They proceeded to show the witness different photographs of robbers, gunmen and a selection of underworld characters who were potential authors of the deed, according to its most salient characteristics. Constrained by his overwhelming sense of confusion, the witness failed to recognize a single face (according to the daily papers).

When the car pulled up in front of them, Spector noted that it was 15.11 by the Town Hall clock.

A tall guy, dressed in a suit, got down from the car and, using both hands, pulled a woman's stocking down over his face, like someone pulling down a blind, and then he leant over the car seat and when he stood up again, he had a machine-gun in his hand. His head was made of rubber, of wax, shapeless, like a honeycomb stuck to his skin causing him to breathe deeply, or to snuffle, from where his voice emerged clipped and artificial. He resembled a wooden dummy, or perhaps a ghost.

'Let's go, Kid,' Dorda said, gasping for breath as if asphyxiating. And to the driver he said: 'We'll be back . . .'

Then Mereles accelerated, and the ready-fitted motor of the Chevrolet, with its racing-car engine and low-slung chassis, roared in the silence of siesta hour, on Town Hall Square, in San Fernando.

The Kid touched the medallion of the Virgin to bring himself luck and got out of the car. He was so thin and fragile and was so drugged that he looked diseased, as if he were a victim of tuberculosis, as they'd told the gunmen beforehand ('sick as a consumptive'), but he earnestly clasped the Beretta .45 in his two hands and when one of the guards moved, he discharged his weapon into his face. The bullet sounded dry, unreal, like a snapped branch.

Dorda had the nylon of the woman's stocking stuck to his face and breathed heavily through the fabric stuck inside his mouth. Off to one side he could see a guy getting down from the truck, and started to fire.

Two old fellows sunbathing on the plaza benches, along with a regular customer, busily perusing his newspaper seated at a table by the bar window opposite, saw how two or three men inside the Chevrolet 400, its plates registered in Buenos Aires province, leapt from the car, weapons in hand.

They seemed enraged, aiming at everyone in sight, sweeping the air in semi-circles as they approached, in slow motion, towards the pick-up. The tallest (according to the witnesses) wore a woman's stocking over his face, but the other one had his features exposed. It was the skinny one with the face of an angel, the one all the witnesses began to call 'the Lad'. He got out of the car, smiled, took aim at the rear end of the pick-up with his machine-gun, then fired off a round.

From the square, one of the retired chaps caught sunbathing saw how the bodies bounced off the seats and the blood splashed off the car windows.

'The fat one was alive when the round was over,' declared one of the old men, 'he tried to open the door and escape and at the same moment saw the guy with a woman's stocking pulled over his head walking along the middle of the road towards the pick-up, and threw himself down on to the pavement.'

He looked like a gigantic bundle, Fatso Spector, thrown against the car and all that in broad sunlight.

Over and again he was convinced they were going to kill

him. He remembered the face of the skinny guy who'd regarded him with a glint of irony. Spector closed his eyes and prepared to die, but felt something like a kick in his chest and was saved by the metal watch his father had left to him. The assailants he managed to catch sight of were two young men dressed in blue suits. Their hair was cropped short, very short, military style. When the firing was over, it was all he could do to run as far as the Bank and ask for help.

Now he was getting nervous, afraid that the police would accuse him of complicity in the handover.

'So you got to see the assailants at close range . . .'

It wasn't a question, but Spector answered it anyway.

'One was dark and the other blond, both were really young and with razored haircuts like soldiers.'

'Describe what you saw.'

He described one. It was Twisty Bazán.

'He was in the bar and then he crossed the square with a pistol in his hand.'

'You mean he was the driver, the one with a stocking over his face, the blond one, and then there was another.'

Spector nodded his head obediently. Had they told him there were four, he would have sworn that indeed, four there were.

The fellow with his face covered by a stocking moved quietly down the middle of the street, and seemed to be smiling, though perhaps this was a grimace induced by the silken mask he had put over his face and tied up on top like a bun. Martínez Tobar was wounded, lying on the floor, doubled over, leaning on his left side, with his briefcase tied to his wrist, and he wasn't able to see when the Kid pulled out the wire-cutters, sliced through the chain and picked up the briefcase with the loot in it, then, as he was moving backwards after all this, fired a shot at his chest. He was equally unable to see when the Gaucho with his stocking-covered face killed the policeman with a shot to the back of the neck.

He'd killed him, that Gaucho Dorda, not because the policeman posed a threat but just because. He killed him because he loathed the police more than anything else in the world and he imagined, in some irrational fashion, that each and every cop he killed would somehow not be replaced. 'One less', was the Gaucho's byword, as if he were reducing the number of troops possessed by an enemy army whose forces would never be renewed. If they carried on killing policemen as a matter of course, at once, without malice, like someone popping off sparrows, those condemned shits of policemen (born with the souls of policemen, souls of hicks), then they'd have to think twice before letting themselves be carried away by their vocation as public executioners, they'd become afraid of getting bumped off in their turn, and thus (he concluded) every day the army of slugs would have fewer troops. So he reasoned, but in a more muddled and lyrical style, as if he were killing cops in a dream, as if he'd been let loose in open countryside with a shotgun; this was the line of thought the Blond Gaucho would follow in his one-man war against the army of slugs.

To kill like that, in cold blood, just because, signified just the opposite (to the police): that these characters would never respect any of the implicit agreements governing the unwritten law between the law and the lawless, that the latter were poisonous, they were thugs, ex-cons, ugly-mug convicts who'd be only too pleased to see the entire police force in Buenos Aires province lined up against a firing squad.

The indescribable confusion produced by this perfidious attack did not make it possible, in the ensuing seconds, to establish precisely what had happened (or so said the daily papers). It was a burst of brutal violence, a blind explosion. An intense battle, lasting just as long as it took for the traffic lights to change. It was over in moments, and afterwards the street was suddenly strewn with corpses.

The shooting at pointblank range caused the death of police agent Otero and fatally wounded the cashier Martínez Tobar in the thorax, also injuring the security guard Balacco in the right leg, before he was dispatched in cold blood by one of the armed men. As for the bank-clerk Spector, stunned and confused, he ran to the Bank to beg for assistance.

Later on it could be confirmed (according to the information given by police officer Silva) that the agent Otero would have been equally unable, even had he emerged unscathed from the attack, to have used his regulation pistol given that one of the bullets fired by the gunmen had lodged in it, putting it out of action. As for the submachine-gun they carried to protect the money while in transit, somebody had put it on a high shelf inside the lorry and nobody could manage to reach it down.

Those who had witnessed the shooting came and went through the place like sleepwalkers, happy to have come through unscathed and horrified at what they had seen. All of a sudden that tranquil afternoon had shown how it could rapidly be transformed into a nightmare.

The burst of bullets unleashed by the assailants also caught Diego García, who was leaving a bar in the immediate neighbourhood of the firing. He was taken to hospital where he died shortly afterwards. He was known to live in Haedo and to have travelled to San Fernando in response to an advert asking for carpenters and cabinet-makers. He had paused at the bar on the square to knock back a glass of gin, and when he left to go and present himself at the sawmill, he was killed by a stray bullet. He was twenty-three years old, and in his pocket were found twelve pesos and a train ticket.

According to one version, armed guards in a building opposite the Town Hall managed to exchange fire with the gunmen, but this remained unconfirmed.

It was noted that one of the assailants was assisted in getting into the car, giving rise to the assumption (according to the police report) that he was wounded. They saw the guy with the masked face throw a white bag, made of canvas, out of the back door of the car as it was already moving and then drop another bag while the Chevrolet set off at full speed for Madero, against the one-way system, towards Martínez Street, in other words towards the city centre of Buenos Aires.

The car was revving at full throttle, running zigzags, hooting its horn at everyone to get out of the way. Two of the gunmen were hanging out of the windows with half their bodies outside, their machine-guns in their hands, firing behind them.

'Give it them round for round, bullet for bullet,' yelled the Kid while Mereles stayed very focused on the driving, crouched forwards, his face pressed up against the windscreen, without any consideration (according to one witness) for the presence of other cars or of the children coming out of school and without waiting for the traffic lights which stopped the cars on the avenue, fixated only on an imaginary line down the street drawing them on to freedom, to the flat on Arenales Street where the Girl was waiting for them, sprawled on the bed studying maths. The Crow was at the wheel of the Chevrolet, and every other car had to get out of the way and let him through.

Everyone in the neighbourhood watched through half-open windows as the black car sped by like a rush of wind. Outside, some of them threw themselves on to the ground, or clustered behind tree-trunks, paralysed with fear, mothers who were on the streets, their children clutching their hands. When people are part of a funeral cortège and look out of the hearse window, they can see those outside removing their hats (should they be wearing hats), slowly and silently crossing themselves as the procession makes its way onwards. The relatives watch the line of people clamped to the wall, along the pavement, who pay their respects, but now from the car it's amusing to observe the disorder (or so the Kid saw it), the idiots throwing themselves to the ground, taking refuge in nearby entrance halls – looking like astonished gargoyles.

'Is it all there?' yelled Mereles, pale in the afternoon light. He held the Chevrolet and crossed the avenue like a sudden draught, still running flat out. He felt the bag beside him without looking at it, and touched the money.

'The loot? Is it all there?' Mereles was laughing.

They hadn't counted it but the canvas bag stuffed with cash was so heavy it could have been filled with stones. Lumps of cement, concealing the fine notes, all in usable currency, packed into a canvas bag tied with a naval knot.

'We were in it up to our necks,' said Dorda.

His shirt was stained with blood, a bullet had grazed his neck, a graze that still burned him. 'But we saved ourselves, Kid, and now we've got to get there,' said the Blond Gaucho, glancing at the Chevrolet's rearview mirror. 'All the dosh in the world.'

He too felt for a bag, then grabbed some powder. They rubbed the cocaine on their gums, they couldn't inhale the stuff at that speed, using their hands like claws to hook out the drug with two crooked fingers from the brown paper bag dangling from the car seat, then rubbing it round their gums and their tongues. Money is just the same as drugs: what's fundamental is its *possession*, knowing it's there, touching it, checking it's still in the cupboard, there in its bag slung among the clothes, checking there's still a half-kilo of the stuff, a hundred grand's worth, being content with that. The first day of the rest of their lives started here.

Nothing can match flying along in a specially tuned car, with double fuel injection and your foot slammed down on the accelerator, the steering wheel stuck to your hands and taking the loot along in the back with you to go and live in Miami or Caracas. That was life at full speed ahead.

'There's a ferry can take us across to Uruguay. It'll take two hours, two hours ten, to cross the pond,' said the Kid.

Was that a question? No one answered. Each one did their own thing and shouted their piece, as if fleeing alone across the countryside on a railway track, with a train bearing down from behind. 'We can go via Colonia and it'll take two hours. Get through Tigre district and, well, we can grab a boat, rent a ferry, buy an aeroplane, eh, darling?' The Kid laughed out loud and took more cocaine with his hand in a claw from the brown paper bag. His tongue and his palate had gone numb, and his voice sounded weird.

'With the acceleration we've got,' said the Gaucho, 'the car could be our ferry.'

'Hey, here's a level-crossing . . . and here's a dead loss of a crossing-keeper.'

'Leave him to me.'

Brignone stuck his body out of the window and, when he saw what he was doing, Dorda did likewise out of the opposite window.

Their machine-gun round sliced through the closed barriers at the level-crossing.

Sparks were flying and wood splintering.

'I had no idea the barriers were so flimsy,' and Kid Brignone laughed out loud.

'They were hanging half outside of the windows and cut clean through,' relayed the crossing-keeper.

Neither the railway employee nor the friend of twenty years who accompanied him could give a coherent description of the assailants, given their state of excitement.

'As they escaped they found the level-crossing barriers closed at Madero Street and without stopping the car they sliced their way across them with a round of machine-gunfire' (according to the papers).

'There were two behind and one in front, with the radio on at full blast. The car was hooting loudly too.'

'The patrolman was following fifty metres behind them.'

'It seems incredible they made their getaway.'

Two guys hanging off the sides of the car with machine-guns in their hands.

According to some witnesses, among the Chevrolet's occupants there seemed to be a wounded man who was being supported by his comrades. In addition, the rear window of the car had been shattered by bullets.

The car came along Libertador Avenue honking its horn

and forcing the traffic to open a path through until, at the crossroads between Libertador and Alvear Avenues, they came across a traffic police substation, which had been put on alert.

Officer Francisco Núñez decided to block the car's path and jumped out into the street but a fresh round of fire burst from the moving car and flung him against a wall. Without pausing in their flight, the yobs let off yet another round of machine-gunfire and peppered the front of the police sub-station.

The Chevrolet shot onwards at full speed with the gunmen still firing off at the police station. Three policemen got into a patrol car and began following them, their siren on at full blast.

Crow Mereles was fully absorbed in his driving. He was addicted to Florinol. He drank the best part of a bottle of the stuff daily, and it lent him a serene vision of life. Florinol is a tranquillizer which, when taken in large doses, functions somewhat like opium; he'd acquired the habit in Batán jail, where it's as obtainable as any legal medicine that doctors can offer on prescription and the nurses can give you in exchange for money or women. The deal was simple: the prisoners' women were far more appealing than the wives of the prison screws and so a market was established, or at any rate a transaction. Visiting hours were really only held to put the young fillies through their paces, as Mereles expressed it. Their fiancées, their girlfriends, the girls who enjoyed whiling away some time with a bit of rough who was up for doing anything to them, would go with a hick if it were required, even with a screw, in short, a no-hope loser who'd take his turn with them in the guards' office. One afternoon the Crow had succeeded in getting his girlfriend at the time, Bimba she was called – sexy all right, but always out of her skull, a total smackhead – to get off with the boss of Batán jail. The guy was nothing but an obese executioner who enjoyed making them all sweat, but whenever he saw the blonde appear, her bottom squeezed tightly into her jeans and wearing a diminutive embroidered T-shirt, he lost the plot. That was what allowed the Florinol and the dope to find their way in. No one could remember any more how exactly the story finished. Or whether or not Bimba carried on with the guy. Either way the Crow made it out of there in six months.

His head emptied itself out, it was carefully vacant, and he could no longer remember what had really happened, but because of that he was an exceptional driver, his mind a blank, and blood so cold that no one could match it. He drove sedated with Florinol and could have faced down a lorry and obliged it to do a U-turn to end up on an embankment. He'd even once gone on an escapade to Mar del Plata in a stolen car with his girlfriend and his girlfriend's mother, and started driving up the wrong side of Highway 2. All the other cars went charging on to the hard shoulder hooting their horns and the Girl laughed aloud and kept taking Vascolet. She – Blanquita – was crazy about the chocolate drink Vascolet (each to their own medicine, Mereles would say, enigmatically). He spoke in a strange manner, taking a while to figure out how to frame his words. By their sounds. His words always sounded serene, even when they were meaningless. Each to their own, but what a screwball, the Girl with her Vascolet!

On arriving at the corner of Libertador Avenue and Aristóbulo del Valle, the luck that had so far accompanied them seemed to run out. At some 150 metres from the military post at Martínez, the Chevrolet launched another round of machine-gunfire in which a policeman was wounded. The gunmen's car (according to the police report) effected a spectacular spin, running a serious risk of doubling back on itself, something it only just managed to avert. The car came to a halt across the street, blocking the traffic, and facing the opposite direction to the one it had been travelling in, coated in the effluent of a broken sewer, its rear window utterly shattered and a large bloodstain on the rear seat. Minutes went by and nobody got out of the car.

Busch, a local shopkeeper, came driving mildly along Libertador Avenue, in a placid frame of mind and from the opposite direction. He spotted the car stopped with its engine running and a man getting down from it rubbing his neck as if he'd been hurt, and imagined that an accident must have taken place.

Señor Eduardo Busch's habits were as regular as the white polka dots printed on the bales of cloth he sold. But today he'd been delayed by two minutes because the water had been cut off while he was washing himself. He hung on under the shower in the growing conviction that someone had it in for him, until he eventually emerged, dried himself, and was informed by his wife that the water had been cut off. He had been born in the same apartment he still lived in and had never gravitated out of the district. He knew all its noises, the shifting movement of the hours, and today it seemed to him he'd heard something unusual (distant thunder, stifled noises) to which he'd paid no attention. He had been out of sorts recently, because things weren't going at all well for him. He always left the house at 2.30 p.m. and at 2.50 p.m. he was opening up his business, but this afternoon he was a little behind and the delay (minimal, just by chance) changed everything. It gave him the opportunity to acquire a story that would last him to the end of his days. When he turned on to Madero Street, he thought there'd been an accident, for he spotted a car with its engine running and a guy getting out with a bag in his hand.

Being by nature a Good Samaritan, he stopped and saw the Kid coming towards him, smiling as he pulled out his Beretta .45 with his left hand.

'He came towards me and I thought he was going to kill me. He took forever to draw level with my car. He looked like a kid but had the face of a desperado.'

The Kid opened the door and Busch got out with his hands up. Two more guys descended from their car and got into the Rambler. They were dragging canvas bags along with them and were heavily armed, but it all happened so rapidly and so confusingly that it seemed like a dream, or so Señor Busch declared. 'We never imagine how these shameful acts come to pass, until we're caught up in them,' he later rationalized, philosophically.

'I'll never abandon the idea that we have to go to the assistance of our neighbour, even when it produces surprises such as this,' he added.

'One was dark and the other blond, the two of them looked very young and had army-style haircuts. There was a third one with a woman's stocking over his head.' All the descriptions converged, to no particular purpose.

They took off in the light-coloured Rambler that he'd bought the previous year. This was the car in which the assailants continued their flight.

They went along Libertador Avenue and after reaching Santa Fe Avenue at top speed – where they miraculously avoided another accident after emerging right into the path of a station wagon – they jumped a set of red lights and headed off along the PanAmerican Highway, the easiest escape route out of the area.

By this stage all the highway police had been alerted, along with all the surveillance divisions along the main routes in and out of the Federal Capital. And the Federal Police's radio command centre had also been switched to high alert.

However, neither the police stations nor the mobile police units covering the wealthy Zona Norte in the city suburbs could keep up with the pace set by the gunmen in their stolen Rambler. A great many provincial police divisions were out that night patrolling a wide swath of Greater Buenos Aires.

# 3

The evening papers carried headline news of the catastrophe. Their first hypotheses invited readers to visualize some kind of commando raid. Investigative journalists associated the robbery with an assault mounted on the Bank's own health centre by a group of nationalists some months previously.*

---

\* In August 1963 a fourteen-man commando unit robbed 14,000 pesos from the Bank's health centre in the district of Caballitos. All fourteen were members of the 'Tacuara gang', who took their name from the prison where they'd done time, in the town of the same name, Entre Ríos province in the northeast of the country. They were also the most

There were, according to their surmises, certain common elements: people from Tacuara or from the Peronist resistance, lower army officers released from the services and now in the employ, if rumours were to be believed, of the Algerian guerrilla movement. 'The Algerians', as they were called in the movement, led by José Luis Nell and Joe Baxter, burst into the health centre waving machine-guns and made off with 300,000 dollars. The police were following a line of investigation in which cells of Peronist nationalists had begun operating alongside common criminals in an explosive combination that was keeping the authorities seriously worried. There was something in it. Hernando Heguilein, 'Nando', a former member of the National Liberation Alliance,* a recognized shock troop during the period of Peronism, had been mentioned together with Malito at the siege on Arenales Street, there to resolve the gang's operational withdrawal and retreat. Nando was a man of action, a patriot in the eyes of some, a 'mole' according to others, a bloodthirsty lumpen proletarian in the view of the police inside the Department.

The daily papers' articles were written between the lines and numerous counter-intelligence operations were covertly running in the midst of the news.

For example, it was revealed that in checking over the Chevrolet left abandoned by the assailants, the police con-

---

dangerous of the extreme right-wing activists in the Peronist movement. On the one hand they were linked to the Arab League and on the other to the Nazi war criminals who had found a safe haven in the Argentine provinces. The common thread lay in violent action and crude anti-Semitism.

firmed their suspicion that one of them had been wounded. From inside the car they recovered: one long-sleeved grey pullover, one hand towel, and one sack, all stained with blood. There were traces of drugs on the car floor, as well as several syringes and a small phial of anticoagulant. As well as all this, they found two 45-calibre double-barrel Halcón sub-machine-guns, each able to take sixty-four bullets, and an unopened case of ammunition. By way of detail illustrative of the assailants' danger to the public (or so said the press), they could point to the fact that each machine-gun had been modified so that the safety catch was jammed with a bolt in the intention that, when it was fired, it emptied whole rounds of fifty bullets at a time. The car itself showed four points of impact on its nearside wing. Next to the site of the accident, and beside the gunmen's car, lay a kit-style bag with 18,000 pesos still inside it. When an examination of the arms left behind in the Chevrolet by the assailants following the car crash was undertaken, it was established that those firing the 9-millimetre machine-gun must have been using a weapon belonging to the same category as a German make, known as a Bergman, or a Paraguayan Piripipi.

According to the most up-to-date reports, the police investigating the bloody assault paid particular attention to the bags abandoned by the malefactors during their flight (some from the crashed Chevrolet, others fallen during the chase). They were made of sailcloth, navy-style, and it was assumed that they were specially manufactured to transport the stolen money. This type of bag is commonly used as military issue. The police made contact with their corresponding numbers in the Naval Prefecture. In addition to all this, the 45-calibre Halcón is a strictly military-issue weapon. It was via this route that an investigation opened into the assumed military connections of the gang.

Inside the car, experts from the Fingerprints Division of the Scientific Police Superintendence dusted for fingerprints supposedly left by the assailants in differing places and on the weapons themselves, and these fingerprints were supposed to lead the investigators to conclusions regarding the identity of the fugitives.

That evening, when the press stories were put to bed, personnel belonging to the Robberies and Larcenies Division conducted a number of house-to-house searches and even house break-ins at various points of the Federal Capital and of Greater Buenos Aires in the search for gang members.

On reading the newspapers, Malito was surprised by the speed with which the police got on their tail. To the typically repulsive and abject style that was their wont (according to Malito), the daily papers now added details intended to embellish the facts in a shamelessly crude and explicit manner ('. . . Andrea Clara Fonseca, six years of age, who let go of her mother's hand, was hit by a hail of machine-gunfire let loose by one of the criminals, and her face was turned into a bloody cavity   '). 'A bloody cavity', Malito returned again to slowly reading that line, without thinking of anything at all, without seeing anything apart from the letters and the blurry image of a fair-haired child resembling a naked cherub in a church. At times, the savage pleasure with which he read the police news convinced him of the impossibility of excavating the moral root of the facts of his life, because in reading about what he himself had done, he felt both satisfied at not having been recognized, and at the same time saddened at not seeing his own photo, while secretly preening himself at this dissemination of his disgrace being anxiously devoured by thousands upon thousands of readers.

Malito was then, like every true gangster, an avid reader of the crime pages of the daily papers, and this was one of his weaknesses, because the primitive sensationalism that cruelly resurfaced in the face of each new crime (the fair-haired girl whose face had been destroyed by gunfire) made him think that his brain was not all that strange when compared with those degenerate sadists who gloat over horrors and catastrophes, made him think his mind was on a level with the minds of those guys who'd done what he read about in the papers, and he secretly thought of himself as one of those criminals, even though in public everyone looked on him as a cold and calculating type, a scientist who organized his actions with the same precision as a surgeon. Naturally, a surgeon (like his father, for example) lived with his hands tainted with blood, ripping open the flesh of naked and defenceless invalids and trepanning away with sophisticated instruments, puncturing and mechanically sawing at the living skulls of his beloved victims.

Abandoning the Chevrolet had been a mistake, and this error gave the police a trail which was enough to provoke a chain reaction, causing all the dominoes to topple in a row. Malito knew that they had broken into the San Fernando hotel where he'd spent the night preceding the assault with Twisty Bazán. Naturally enough, the police weren't revealing any information they'd obtained there.

In a manner at once threatening and indifferent, the police announced they knew the identity of at least two of the gang members. Or so the second chief of the Robberies and Petty Larcenies Division of the Zona Norte in the province of Buenos Aires, Cayetano Silva, assured the press.

'I am leaving aside the possibility that a degree of internal collusion with personnel at the Town Hall may have taken place *a priori*,' declared Police Commissioner Silva.

They were putting up a smokescreen, to protect their line of information. Malito had the feeling that they were already waiting there on his doorstep. Things never work out as you expect them to, and luck is more important than courage, more important than intelligence and security measures. Fortune, paradoxically, always favours the side of the established order of things and is (along with denunciation and torture) the principal means by which investigators can close the loop and finally snare those who attempt to render themselves invisible in the urban jungle.

Despite the elected muteness of the police chiefs, it soon transpired that there was a firm trail leading the investigators towards the gang's political contacts. Nor should one rule out the possibility that the gunmen had been contracted to act as decoys, as the visible elements in a far larger organization. Unofficially, there was talk of an operation maintained by the clandestine network of the so-called Peronist resistance. The police firmly inquired after all the locations visited by former militants in the organization led by Marcelo Queraltó and Patricio Kelly.*

Hernando Heguilein, Nando, had been loosening his ties with circles of Peronist nationalism and only maintained sporadic contact with certain militant trade unionists and former combatants of the movement dedicated to arms trafficking, renting safehouses and supplying secret workshops

---

* Founders of the National Liberation Alliance (ALN).

where passports and false documents could be manufactured (along with faked letters from Perón invoking an armed uprising). Here he was, driving along Boedo in a Chevrolet with all his papers in order, attempting to make any number of turns before heading off towards the bachelor pad on Arenales Street. He didn't want to phone them, nor to arrive early, because, like all the rest of them circling the city with the police hard on their tails, he was scared of falling into a bear pit, of accepting a poisoned chalice, or of falling into a trap, with the cops hanging out in the apartment. On various occasions Nando had managed to avert disaster, purely by instinct, because he took signs of unusual activity very seriously and responded very methodically, to consistently achieve the most satisfactory outcome.

He descended via Santa Fe, turned along Bulnes Street, and carried on for another half a block. There was a young couple canoodling against a tree and some guy reading a paper in a cab parked at the taxi rank at Berutti Street. The entrance to the building was reasonably quiet and the caretaker was sluicing down the paving stones. It was a good sign: porters make themselves scarce when the police are about to turn up. Half the porters in Buenos Aires belonged to the Communist Party and the other half were stool-pigeons, but not one of them was to be found whenever the cops set an ambush. Which explains Nando's conviction that the caretaker hosing down the pavement could as well have been a cop in camouflage, ready to shop him the instant he got in the lift.

Nando meandered along with a peaceful air, went into the hall, and down to the basement giving on to the garage. There was no one there. He crossed the corridor and went up the service staircase. He preferred to enter via the kitchen, for if the cops were already inside, he had a chance (however remote) of entrenching himself in the incinerator chute and defending himself with bullets.

But there were no policemen, everything was fine as he crossed the kitchen and went into the living-room, where the first thing he saw was Blond Gaucho stretched out across a sofa, with a bloodied bandage around his neck, and the Kid filing down the firing-pin on his piece, very carefully, on a rattan coffee table. Most amusing of all was the money piled up on a kind of inlaid Spanish cabinet with a mirror that duplicated its quantity, a heap of dosh on a white oilcloth, an hallucinatory spectacle, repeated in the pure waters of the mirror.

The Kid looked at it and gave a complicit grin, while the Gaucho gestured towards the closed bedroom door through which suffocated grunts and sexual groans were emerging. It had to be the Crow and the Girl, whiling away their lives there in bed.

'Malito's here,' said the Kid and nodded towards the room at the end. Then he went back to filing the firing-pin on his Beretta, trying to get the trigger as docile and sensitive to the touch as a butterfly. He didn't like Nando, he was cut from another block, resembling a cop, with his trimmed moustache and dead eyes. But he wasn't a real cop, although he had been a sort of one, an informer on the Alliance. 'Let's call him a political activist,' the Kid was sizing him up, a fool like any other, who would have themselves killed for the Old Man, in the end the most poisonous of all were those who joined with their fellows (or so they said) to resell arsenals of weaponry and raid banks under the pretext of raising funds for Perón's return. 'The Return, cabbage-heads,' thought the Kid, 'the only thing we have in common is that they pinch us to find out whether we're Peronist trade union puppets or not.'*

'Any news?'

'All going well,' said Nando. 'Shooting their mouths off without a clue about what's really what. They went and put Big Pig Silva in charge, he's a sly one, you need to watch out, he must be putting the squeeze on all the narks, and by this stage he'll have to have a lead from somewhere. Did you see the papers? Losing that car was a disaster. Were you the one who picked it up?'

'The Crow went. He collected it in Lanús, no fuss, it was a heavily modified job the cops had sold to a metal merchant. It was already marked.'

Nando warned them they'd need to spend two or three days locked indoors, lying low, until they'd sorted out the deal to get them across the River Plate. The Gaucho lowered the magazine he was reading and peered over the top.

'You're not Uruguayan, are you?'

They gazed at one another for a moment in silence and Nando shook his head.

'I'm not Uruguayan, but I'll get you over to Uruguay.'

'I know that, of course, but you have the look of a native,† you know, you sort of give the impression . . .' burbled the

---

* 'The Old Man': in his period of exile, in 1965, Perón was already seventy years old. He would make a triumphant return to office in 1973, dying six months later. The CGT (Confederación General de Trabajadores) was the Peronist-controlled Trades Union Congress.
† Lit. a *charrúa*, of an 'indian' tribe north of the River Plate.

Gaucho. 'All Uruguayans look as if they've been widowed . . .
The truth of the matter is, they all look like Peronists,
Uruguayans do, all widows of the General.'

'You're a nice guy, Gaucho. What's up with you?' commented Nando. 'You've launched into speech, have you, now
that you're feeling better?'

The Gaucho raised his newspaper again and resumed
reading.

Nando spoke like this to him because the Gaucho was a
man of few words, and got along with the Kid without the use
of them. They'd often spend hours alone together, without
speaking, thinking and listening to things. He could hear a
kind of murmuring in his head, a short-wave radio attempting to infiltrate the plates of his skull, transmitting via the
inner part of the brain, something along those lines.

At times there'd be an interference, strange sounds, people
talking in unknown languages, chattering simultaneously,
who knows whether from Japan, Russia, whatever. It didn't
bother him too much because it had been going on ever since
he was a boy. Other times it annoyed him, for example when
he was trying to get to sleep, or when all at once phrases
entered his head and he had to spit them out. Like just now,
when he'd told Nando he was a Uruguayan widow. He'd
heard it in the bones of his skull, he'd spat it out, and then the
guy had looked at him strangely. He was not wanting to cause
problems, and at the same time amusing himself thinking of
what a turnip-head Nando was when he told him he had the
aspect of a *charrúa*, a native Uruguayan. And the oddity of the
word 'aspect' likewise evoked a grin in him. It sounded as if
someone had told Nando he had a 'prospect' or an 'insect'.
Something medicinal. So, he awarded himself an ampheta-

mine, an Actemin. Nando and the Kid carried on chatting, but the Gaucho scarcely heard them, it was like the wind in the trees. He sat down on the bed and listened.

'Che,'* said Nando, looking first at the Kid and then at the closed door. 'Is Malito still in there?'

Malito was still in there, locked into the other room, the Venetian blinds pulled well down to screen out the sun's rays, in twilight, but with a bedside lamp on, shaped like a tulip and with a 25-watt bulb. Because he couldn't bear to go to sleep in darkness, after all those years in prison with the light on all night long, a little habit from the years in his cell. Nando had got to know Malito in the Sierra Chica prison back in '56 or '57, and remembered him as a reserved sort of lad, very young, who'd fallen into political hands as if by mistake. They'd tortured the lot of them as if it were an initiation ritual. Those were the tough days of the resistance, and Malito found himself on a block along with Communists and Trotskyists and the Nazis from the National Restoration Vanguard. He got into fights with them: there were a number of members of the Metallurgy trade union, two or three former army officers and a few guys from the Tacuara barracks. Malito and Nando became mates. It was from then you could date their unlikely alliance, founded on long hours of conversation through the dead prison nights. Both highly intelligent, they rapidly learnt from one another and as rapidly set about drawing up plans.

---

* 'Che' – Ernesto Guevara notwithstanding – is not a proper name. It's what every Argentine male informally calls another. Something like 'mate'.

'Any group who's daring enough can do a lot in a country like this,' Nando was wont to say. 'There's swindlers all over the place. A highly disciplined and ordered group, a band of well-armed spivs can achieve anything here.' And here was where they were. He thought it best to gather together an armed gang of insiders rather than go outside and recruit people he'd need to train up.

Nando dreamed of bringing them into the Organization. Laying pipe-bombs, robbing banks, cutting electric cables, starting fires, raising hell. But things worked out otherwise and it was the old swindling insiders who ended up making Nando their Organizer. He was gifted with clearsightedness, and a strategic perspective. It was he who'd provided the necessary intelligence to mount a raid on the Bank. He had umpteen contacts which he'd used to establish the essential lines of withdrawal and retreat after the operation. He knew everyone, and he knew how to operate. He'd obtain the falsified documents, the necessary shipments, the Uruguayan contacts, and provide bribes and the outlets for selling on arms. He was at the heart of everything and was planning a secret crossing to Uruguay. But there were still many problems to be resolved before making a move. And Nando wasn't in favour of getting mixed up with the police and the informers who made the handover during the raid.

Malito sat down on the bed and lit a cigarette: all the weapons were spread out on the table, and the newspapers were strewn around the floor. He'd no desire to share out the loot, not with the narks, nor with the cops.

'You're daft, they'll denounce you straight away.'

'Nando, if I were to hand over half the cash to those idiots who didn't lift a finger while we risked our bollocks,' here Malito grinned, 'then I really would be daft.'

The situation was confused; the police were attempting to disguise what they knew, they appeared disorientated and followed their established tendency to link the assault to Peronist right-wing factions. Was that where they were looking? Nando wasn't sure, though he knew Silva the Big Pig well enough. Police Commissioner Silva, from Robberies and Larceny, didn't believe in investigating, he simply went for torture and denunciation as his chosen methods. (As soon as they were detained, the gunmen knew to cut themselves with razors, on their forearms and legs, to prevent the cattle prods being used on them. 'If there's blood there's no cattle prod, because you'd collapse instantly from the electric current.') He'd mounted a death squad on the Brazilian model. But Silva always acted within the law, always with the backing of the Federal Police, because his working hypothesis was that every crime had a political significance. 'Common criminality no longer exists,' Silva was wont to wax lyrical. 'Nowadays all our criminals are ideological ones. It's the legacy that Peronism bequeathed us. Any young thug you catch in the act of thuggery automatically shouts "Long live Perón!" or "Evita still lives!" when you go to snatch him. They're all social delinquents, terrorists who get up in the middle of the night, leave their women asleep in bed, take the number 60 bus, get out somewhere near a level-crossing and blow up a train. If, like the Algerians, they're at war with the whole of society, they'll be wanting to kill the lot of us.' This was the reason (according to Silva) why you had to coordinate police activity with the State Intelligence Service and purge the shit from the city.

Cold, intelligent, a real professional, well trained but utterly fanatical, that Commissioner Silva. He had his own weird personal history which nobody knew too well: according to some, a daughter of his had been killed in an attack on her way home from school; according to others, his wife had been rendered paralysed (when she was thrown down a lift-shaft); still others claimed he'd taken a bullet in the balls and been left impotent; all these stories and more ran in various versions. He was paranoid, he never slept; he had a number of extravagant notions as to the political future and the advance of Communism and of the vulgar masses. He always gave the correct line, advancing some set-piece argument or other, offering detailed digressions by way of explanation. Those in the Peronist resistance (resumed Silva), weary of militant heroics, had begun to take their own direct action. It was vital to sever this connection, or else the bad old days when the anarchists held sway would return, when no one could distinguish the crooks from the politicians. The gallant criminal divisions of Buenos Aires province had been waging a campaign of extermination. They killed all they encountered bearing arms and took no prisoners. And they'd encountered only support from the head of Federal Police, who saw only a call to Armageddon in every strike threat.

'Silva smells a rat in everything that happens. He'll hang on a little longer because he wants to be certain, but his staff is stuffed with stoolies who keep him abreast of things . . .'

'Have you lot spoken to him?'

'We've got people in the Head Office and we know what they're up to, but Silva only talks to himself, never even to his own mother. Get the picture?' inquired Nando.

'Yup,' replied Malito. He was evidently worried. 'Call the Crow.'

The Crow emerged from the nest where he was bedbound with the Girl, then went over and shut himself in the room with Malito and Nando. After a while he came out, wearing a bored expression.

'Come on in, Kid,' he said and stared at the Gaucho. Malito says that you're his eyes and ears, observing everything from the balcony overlooking the street.'

Dorda was wounded in the neck, not seriously, but a bullet had rebounded off his pistol butt and hit the nape of his neck. He began bleeding heavily and everyone assumed he was going to die, but in a few hours the wound began to scab over and he began to look better. But he was weakened by the considerable loss of blood and the Kid had been looking after him.

'What's up?'

'Nothing. I'll let you know.'

Dorda didn't move. He stared at Kid Brignone, who stuck his pistol in his belt and also went through into the other room.

'Up you get, Gaucho,' said the Crow from the doorway. 'And keep watch over the lovenest.'

Gaucho Dorda remained alone in the room. Without shifting from his position on the sofa, he searched out the bottle of amphetamines, swallowing two of them without water. They on their side of the door were hatching plots. They didn't speak to him, they never asked him anything. The Kid was in charge of making plans. As far as the Gaucho was concerned, he and the Kid were one and the same. Twinned brothers, identical twins, belonging to the mafia fraternity, meaning (here Dorda struggled to explain him-self) they understood each other without words, they acted telepathically. It even seemed to him that he felt the same way as Kid Brignone. That was why Dorda left the daily timetable to be settled by the Kid. Money and decision-taking mattered little to him. His sole interest was in drugs, 'his obscure pathological mentality' (according to the report by Dr Bunge, the prison psychiatrist), he rarely thought of anything else apart from drugs and the voices to which he paid secret attention. It was logical (again according to Dr Bunge) that the Gaucho would leave all the decisions to the Kid. 'A very interesting case of Gestalt symbiosis. There may be two of them, but they function as a single entity. The Gaucho acts as the body, solely responsible for executing the action, a psychotic killer; the Kid is the brains and does the thinking for him.'

However, he also heard voices, the Blond Gaucho. Not all the time, but from time to time, he heard voices, inside his head, between the plates of his skull. Women addressing him, issuing commands. That was his secret and Dr Bunge deter-mined it was necessary to give him various tests and various sessions of hypnotherapy so that the themes of this intimate music might be drawn out. Dr Bunge became obsessed with this case, became struck by these voices his prisoner-patient Dorda listened to in silence. 'They tell me there's a lagoon up near Carhué, and that if you throw yourself into the water, there's so much salt in it you float, and they say that there some bastard chieftain met his death, a Ranquel indian* who drowned there when they tied a millstone to his neck, 'cause they said he fucked some poor gringo he'd caught and chained to a post by the ankle, that indian went and did it to him over on the indian settlement, this Coliqueo chief I'm telling you about. And they drowned him in the lake. Ever since then the poor devil appears from time to time, floating on the surface still dressed in his plumes, and the current carries him away through the marshes between the flatlands of rushes and reeds like a ghost.' Then his voice would go all lethargic and he'd repeat, the Blond Gaucho, a fragment from the Holy Bible (Matthew XVIII: 6) which a priest had read to him: 'And whomsoever should scandalize a white man, were it better for him that a millstone were hanged about his neck and that he be drowned in the depth of the lagoon at Carhué.'

Apart from the voices, he was a regular sort of guy. On occasions even Dr Bunge thought he was faking it, this Dorda, looking to escape from the law by feigning madness and avoiding a sentence. In any case, Dr Bunge wrote in his report that Dorda's 'characterpathology' had all the indications of a behavioural aberration, with a tendency towards aphasia. Because he heard voices he spoke little: they were the explanation for his taciturnity. Those who avoid speech, for example the autistic, are always hearing voices, people talking to them, they live on another frequency, preoccupied by the hubbub, an interminable muttering, listening to instructions, shouts, suffocated giggles, receiving orders. (Sometimes they called him 'the Slapper', these voices, all these women, calling

---

* Ranquel or Mapuche tribes are, literally, 'people of the swamp', who settled in the northwest Pampa and south of Córdoba in the seventeenth and eighteenth centuries. The Coliqueo 'indians' settled southwest of San Luis.

to Gaucho Dorda, 'Come here Slapper, Slag, Bitch,' and he kept quiet, without moving, so that nobody could hear what they were saying to him, sadly gazing into space, occasionally longing to cry but without giving in so that no one would ever discover that he was a woman.) He took the greatest pride in his decision-taking and in maintaining sang-froid. Nobody could read his mind, or hear what his women said to him. He sported a brand of sunglasses called Clipper, with reflective lenses, he'd found them in a glove-pocket one afternoon when he was robbing a posh car out near leafy Palermo. He liked them, found them elegant, they afforded him a worldly air and he looked at himself in profile in the mirror, in every bathroom, in every shop window.

Right now he removed his Clippers, and with extreme care began perusing the design of an outboard motor on a launch drawn to scale. He was still sprawled across the sofa, studying a magazine called *Popular Mechanics*, and pausing now and then to draw engines. He sat down and placed a sheet of kitchen paper on the side table and began tracing with the tip of his pencil.

At that moment the Girl appeared, dressed in a man's shirt, and went barefoot into the kitchen.

'Want something, Doll?' asked the Gaucho.

'Nothing, thanks,' replied the Girl and the Gaucho watched as her shirt lifted above her arse while she stood on tiptoes to reach down the dope from the top shelf of the kitchen dresser.

'Give us a kiss,' asked Dorda.

The Girl paused in the doorway and gave him a smirk. She treated him as if he were invisible, or made of wood. He could see the little curls of pubic hair beneath the folds of the Crow's silk shirt, he could see the Girl's – the Doll's – pubis.

He visualized the soft rub of the silk between her legs and couldn't stop staring at her.

'What are you looking at? Just wait till I tell Daddy about you,' said the Girl and she went back into her room.

The Gaucho made as if to get himself up and follow her, but fell back across the cushions, with a faint smile on his face. When he was annoyed, he beamed like a child.

He looked at the closed door through half-screwed eyes, he was all screwed up over screwing and had a convergent squint (as his late mother put it), which enhanced his appearance as a highly dangerous obsessive type, which is what he was (according to Dr Bunge's report).

Dorda thus possessed the perfect look of the category of subject he represented (added Dr Bunge), a criminal lunatic who performed criminal deeds with a nervous smile, angelical and soullesss. When he was a boy, his late mother surprised him chopping a live chick in half with a shearing blade, and she removed him from the henhouse to the police station, whipping him with a leather strap, to have him banged up at Longchamps.

'My very own mother!' he stammered, without knowing whether to curse or to thank her for her efforts at straightening out his life. 'Wickedness,' said Dorda, flying high on the mixture of speed and coke, 'is not something that happens with intention, it's a bright shining light that comes and carries you away.'

He was repeatedly detained as a child, and at the age of fifteen they sent him to the Melchor Romero neuropsychiatric clinic, near to La Plata. The youngest sectioned inmate in its entire history he'd proudly say, Dorda would. They sat him down in a white room with the other crazies and he hardly reached up to the table. But he was a veritable Judas, a child criminal: he killed cats by putting them into wasps' nests. A very complex operation.

'I don't want to boast,' the Gaucho said, 'but I made some wire cages so secure that the kitten couldn't move, it could only cry and squawk like a hen. The pussycat.'

Soon afterwards he killed a hobo, with his fists, in order to steal his torch. First off they took him to the police station, where they beat him to a pulp, then they sectioned him in the psychiatric hospital.

The doctor on duty was a bald fellow with glasses who wrote notes in an exercise book. He sent him to a unit for non-aggressive crazies and the first night he was raped by three male nurses. One made him suck him off, the next held him down, and the third stuffed him up the arse.

'A dick as big as this,' Dorda indicated the size with his hands. 'And I don't want to boast, or anything.'

He became meat for the madhouse. He'd escape and they'd recapture him, he'd escape again and roam around the train stations, through Retiro or Once, living off petty crimes and hold-ups, burgling empty houses. From the moment he spotted a car to when he took it out, he needed just two minutes, maximum two and a half. The fastest draw in the West, because he kept his patch to Morón or Haedo (on the west of the city). He came from the countryside and was always drawn to the city outskirts. He had the ruddy face of a peasant, straw-coloured hair, sky-blue eyes. He was a provincial from the provinces, from a family of Piedmontese immigrants at María Juana in the Santa Fe province, hard-working people, as taciturn as he but who didn't hear voices. According to his mother, evil came to him as naturally, and he welcomed it with the same force and obstinacy, as hard work to his father and his brothers.

'Out in the countryside, the sun's fit to fry your brains. The birds fall from the trees with the summer heatwave. You don't earn anything with the sweat of your labours,' the Gaucho Dorda decided. 'The more you work, the less you have, my youngest brother had to sell his house when his wife fell ill and he'd worked hard his whole life long.'

'Of course he did,' the Kid laughed aloud. 'Maybe the idiot's getting wise: the more you work, the more of a slave you become . . .'

Kid Brignone and Gaucho Dorda, forever together, had got to know one another in Batán jail, that old heap of shit, both happening to end up in a unit filled with faggots. Whores, trannies, queens . . . the whole selection box.

'The first time a man queered me, I thought I'd get pregnant,' said Dorda. 'Let's see if I'll go for the op now. I was still a kid when I first saw his stiffie and I thought I'd faint with delight.' He laughed loudly and pulled a stupid face. Dorda was acting the clown, making Malito nervous, he the pro, disliking coarse jokes, disliking rent boys. According to Malito, all whores talked too much.

But that wasn't true, the Kid protested, there were queens who'd lasted through torture sessions with the cattle prod without singing, and he personally knew several who played the macho and as soon as they saw the rubber straps began to sing aloud.

'Mad Margarita, a trannie, filled her gob with razor blades and made a real mess of her mouth, and when she stuck her tongue out at the cops she said: "If you want, I'll suck it for you, sweetheart, but you'll never get me to squeal . . ."

'They killed her and had to throw her in the river at Quilmes, completely naked but for her bracelet and ear-rings, but they never did get a word out of her.'

'You have to be all male to get yourself fucked by a macho,' decided Gaucho Dorda. And he smiled like a child, cooler than a cat. There was one guy he planted a darning needle into a lung of, the fellow went *whishsh*, the air went out of him like a balloon and he was left completely deflated. They called him Mental. And Gaucho didn't like being called Mental, or being called Menial. The Blond Gaucho demanded more respect. 'I've been a lost soul from the very start,' and he smiled like a girl.

The Kid immediately clocked that the Gaucho was highly intelligent, but completely off his head.

'Psychotic,' added Dr Bunge, chief headshrinker at Melchor Romero.

That was why he heard voices. Those who kill for killing's sake do it because they hear voices, they hear people talking, they're in contact with the energy exchange, with the voices of the dead, with lost women, 'it sounds like a humming,' said Dorda, 'an electric buzz you can hear going cric, cric inside your brains, that doesn't let you get to sleep.'

'You suffer a thousand martyrdoms, you madman, with that radio always playing in your head, you know what that means. They talk to you, they tell you all kinds of obscenities.'

The Kid worried about the Blond Gaucho and looked after and defended him. He picked him for the assault on San Fernando. Malito called him because he'd carefully observed the Kid and needed a heavyweight from the next generation, he wanted to renew the team, enough of old fogeys ('For old fogeys you can stop at me,' Malito would say, having recently celebrated his fortieth.) He put the job his way, and the Kid responded with: 'If we go fifty fifty with the cops, how much do we end up taking home?'

'Minimum, half a million . . . divided between four of us.'

'And the other half-million?'

'It's theirs,' said Malito.

'They' were those who set up the deal, including the cops and those on the Town Council. The Kid gave this some thought. He delayed reaching a decision. They were on borrowed time: if he got caught again he would never get out.

'I'll come in with the Blond Gaucho as my second. Otherwise count me out.'

'Who d'you think you are?' asked Malito. 'Man and wife?'

'Of course, cretin,' answered the Kid.

When the flesh urged they shared a bed, the Kid and the Blond Gaucho, but generally less and less. Dorda was a semi-mystic: he preferred to let himself be taken and didn't jerk off because he was deeply suspicious. He thought that if he lost his juices, he'd lose what little light still illuminated his mind, and he'd be left high and dry, without an idea in his head.

'I'm up to here with playing Little Bo Peep. Seriously, doctor,' Gaucho told the doctor, as though it was a heavy load to bear, 'when you're banged up by the cops, what are you to do? Do it to yourself every half-hour like a monkey . . . or like a dog licking itself, haven't you noticed, doctor? Dogs lick themselves off, in Devoto jail there was a guy from Entre Ríos who could suck himself off, he doubled over like a piece of wire, stuck out his tongue and sucked away . . .' the Gaucho was laughing.

'Well and good, Dorda,' answered Dr Bunge. 'That'll be all

for today.' And he noted on his pad: 'Sexual obsession, poly-morphous perversion, uncontrolled libido. Dangerous, psychotic, perverted. Parkinson's Disease.'

The Gaucho had a slight tremor, electric and almost imper-ceptible, but he explained it away with his schema of aerated and corporal humours.

'We are composed of air,' he declared. 'Skin and air. Beyond this, inside ourselves, everything is all wet, wetness covers everything between skin and air,' he was attempting to explain things scientifically this Blond Gaucho, 'and there are some little tubes . . .'

This vision of man as a balloon was confirmed to him when he saw the guy he'd pricked with a darning needle deflate and fall to the floor like clothes dropped there at the end of the day. The guy, on the floor, like so much dirty wash-ing.

'We're made of spunk, air and blood,' announced the Gaucho, one night when he was flying on coke and loquacity.

'He was full of words,' recalled and recounted the Kid, 'he'd swallowed a load of first-class stuff we'd lifted from the car glove compartment of a deputy in the National Assembly.'

'There are these little tubes,' went on Dorda, and here he pointed to his chest, 'going from here to there,' and he fin-gered his way around his ribcage. 'Like, made of plastic, they are, and they empty and refill, empty and refill. When they're filled, you think, and when they're empty, you sleep. If you remember something, like back when you were a kid, it's because those things, memories or whatever, happened to be out there in the air, they just came along, didn't they, those things you remember, blowing in the wind, right there for you to catch. Am I right, Kid?'

'Naturally,' Brignone said to him, letting him be right.

Highly intelligent, that Dorda, if very locked in on himself, with that problem of his, aphasia, that dumbness which meant he didn't speak for a month on end, communicating simply with signs and gestures, rolling his eyes to the skies, or pursing his lips to make himself understood. Only the Kid could understand him, that loony Gaucho. But he was the most complete and courageous guy you could ever wish to see (according to Brignone). There was the time he confronted the police with a .9 and he held them at bay until the Kid could get there with a car jammed in reverse and pull him out, in Lanús. It was awesome. Stock still, firing with both hands, serenely – bang, bang – even elegantly, and the cops shitting themselves with fear. When they come across a character like that, decisive, who doesn't give a fart, they give him respect. 'If there'd been a war, let's just suppose, say he'd been born in the time of General San Martín,* that Gaucho,' or so the Kid proposed, 'they'd have erected a monument to him. He'd have been I dunno what, some kind of a hero, but he was born out of his time. He has this problem about expressing himself, which makes him very introverted. Perfect for carrying out special assignments. He'll go and kill off anyone, and do it in the blink of an eye. Once, during a robbery, the cashier wasn't prepared to play along with it, thought it was some sort of a game, and he acted like a fool, the cashier did,

---

* San Martín was the liberator of the Southern Cone from Spanish rule, and a brilliant military strategist. The most famous equestrian statue in Buenos Aires is dedicated to him, in the park at the centre of the Plaza San Martín.

in that bank, 'cause he couldn't see a gun, 'cause the Gaucho wasn't showing his weapon.

'So he said: "This is a raid."

'And the prick of a cashier, when he saw him there, looking like a mental defective, thought it was all a joke, and that he was fooling. "Get out," he said. Or "Stop fucking with me, dumbo," he might have said. Dorda scarcely moved his hand, just slightly like this, inside the pocket of his white coat (because he'd put on a medic's, one he'd taken from the hospital) and he emptied the chamber into the guy's face.

'The bank staff themselves all rushed to fill his bag when they saw him smiling broadly after stiffing the guy, the cashier guy. A very, very heavy guy, Gaucho Dorda, a total loony. They don't beat him up either, the cops, don't put him through their paces. You might as well kill him, for all the talk you'll get out of him.'

'You remind me of a fellow I picked up once in the Retiro station, in the toilet – did I tell you this one, Gaucho? – a fellow like you, I was peeing, the guy was circling me, staring at my thing, circling me again, so then I began making small talk and the fellow held out a sheet of paper which read: *I'm deaf-and-mute*. So I did it anyway. And he paid me 150 pesos. He breathed heavily while he was shafting me, 'cause of course he couldn't say anything, but he let out his breath, exhaled, enjoying it.'

'I'm deaf-and-mute too,' the Kid went on and burst out laughing and the Gaucho gazed at him contentedly, before he too uttered a disturbed little cackle.

Dorda remembered it, and he also loved the Kid. He couldn't say as much, but he was willing to give his life for Brignone. Right now he made an effort, and got up. It was hard work thinking, but he was doing it and his mind was running on like a translation machine (according to Dr Bunge), everything seemed directed personally to upset him (well, him or the Brignone Kid). They spoke to him and he translated. For example, when he was a boy, he used to attend the church cinema, since he, Dorda, was from the countryside, and in the country cinema is a religious devotion. 'If you went to Mass,' (recounted the Gaucho) 'the priest would give you, when you left, a ticket (and if you'd taken communion, the priest would give you two) which got you in free to the parish cinema, which was showing after morning mass.' Dorda could get to see even a whole series of films and translated every one, as if he were on screen, as if he'd lived it all himself. ('Once we had to take him out of the screening, because he pulled out his willy and began weeing: in the film he could see a child urinating, his back to the audience, urinating in the night, in the middle of the countryside . . .': deposition from the sacristan to Dr Bunge, included in his psychiatric report.) A devout believer, Dorda, always wishing to remain in God's grace, and his mother went so far as to declare that he had wanted to become parish priest at Del Valle (a village some five kilometres away from his family home) where the Brothers of the Sacred Heart were based, but when he was on his way to visit, a hobo stopped and took advantage of him, and from that time stemmed all his many misfortunes.

At that moment, Mereles came out of the room.

'What are you up to, dickhead?' he asked the Gaucho, who seemed to be in a dream. 'Come on. We've got to go down and make a phone call.'

They'd decided not to pay out and to stuff everyone else. That was why Malito had determined to change plans and get

him to ring Twisty Bazán. It was six o'clock on the Thursday
morning. He didn't let him tell Twisty where they were holed
up, but he sent him along to meet Fontán Reyes in a bar on
Carlos Pellegrini and Lavalle, so as to keep him occupied
while they shifted themselves to the other safehouse. He gave
the order to depart and regroup at Nando's house over in
Barracas. That was where they intended to wait until the new
network was in place to get them over to Uruguay.

Tall, skinny, with his vulture's eyes and a superior smile on
his lips, Twisty Bazán was arrested three hours after the call.
To cover himself, Silva said Bazán had been detained in the
vicinity of the square where the robbery had taken place. He
had a weapon on him. He said he was carrying the gun 'to kill
the stray dogs that have overrun Hurlingham'. The truth is he
was a police informer. Silva had had him hooked for over a
year as a nark, in return for leaving him free to circulate the
Bajo among the drugs and the whores.

# 4

Next day the newspapers carried pictures of Police Commissioner Silva in the act of identifying the corpse of Twisty Bazán in a bar beside the harbour. His pronouncements were both sententious and contradictory (mutually incompatible, even), as befits a perfect example of police logic.

'In this country criminals fall to killing one another in order to avoid coming to justice. We are on the trail of the gang of assassins who robbed the San Fernando bank and their hours are now numbered.'

The commissioner wore a crumpled suit and had a

bandage on one hand. He'd not slept for two nights and had fractured his hand hitting Mereles' harlot, who had refused to cooperate and spent the entire interrogation spitting and swearing. She was only a kid, a real brat set on playing the heroine, and in the end he'd had to hand her over to the judge with almost nothing to show for his efforts. He'd broken a bone in his knuckle in throwing the first punch and his hand was now swollen and painful. He asked for ice at the bar and tied the cubes into a white napkin to hold against it. Then he turned to glower at the journalists.

'You wouldn't happen to think . . .' began the lad who wrote up the police reports for *El Mundo*.

'I don't think, I investigate,' Silva cut him short.

'They say he was a police informer.' The lad was really only a curly-haired boy, wearing his press pass on the lapel of his corduroy jacket, which clearly read Emilio Renzi or Rienzi. 'And they also say that he'd been pulled in and detained . . . Who gave the order to release him?'

Silva glowered again, holding his wounded hand to his chest. Of course it was he who'd released Twisty to use him as bait.

'He's a criminal with a police record. And he was never detained . . .'

'What's happened to your hand, police commissioner?'

Silva struggled to find a reply that would appear convincing to the lad in front of him.

'I put it out when I was thumping fucking journalists in the balls.'

Commissioner Silva was a fat fellow, with proletarian features, a white scar blazed across one cheek. The story of his scar returned to him every morning when he looked at his face in the mirror. A madman had cut him one evening, just because, as he was leaving his house. The bastard breathed down his neck and threatened him with a blade, without realizing that he was a cop. When he did realize it, matters only got worse. The problem is always the other party's fear, the delirium of some guy who reckons he's been cornered and that there's no way out for him. They went on out on to the street and, before taking his car, the fellow opened his face with a diagonal slit. It was as if he'd been burned, he felt an icy fire, something slashed his jaw and he was left with a permanent scar.

These days he lived alone, his wife had left him years earlier and occasionally they'd meet up and he'd hardly recognize her when she sometimes brought the children over. He watched them grow up with indifference, as if they were strangers; alienated from anything that wasn't about work. Silva knew that in his job you couldn't beat about the bush. And this time he'd kept his hands free.

'This time there needs to be a swift outcome,' his boss had told him. 'You've *carte blanche* not to worry about what the judges may have to add to the proceedings.'

There was a lot of pressure to bring about an arrest.

'I'm up to here with journalists, and I'll have to call a press conference.'

'You got any clues?'

Commissioner Silva set off by car for Entre Ríos Street via Moreno Street, outside working hours. It was nearly nine at night. He drove calmly. The city was quiet. Crime, robbery, adultery, everything taking place, so you go about your business, you hit the streets and it all looks normal, has that false air of tranquillity that the other passers-by themselves bestow.

Silva would often stay up until dawn, at home, without being able to get to sleep, staring out at the city through the window, in the dark. Everyone tries to cover up evil. But evil lies in wait around every corner, and within every house. He now lived in a top floor flat on Boedo Street and the lights burned in houses and apartments through the dawn, reminding him of all the crimes that would be front-page news in the next morning's dailies.

Twisty's execution was the last straw that signalled the gang's retreat. The lesson couldn't have been plainer: they were going to kill anyone who stood in their way, or whom they had the good fortune to pull in. Nando Heguilein had remained in the rearguard, covering their final moves and distributing the money to cover the crossing to Uruguay. Everything was going badly and smelt of danger; the police raiding and requisitioning the safehouse on Arenales Street and then Blanca's capture – she was there in the house – enraged Mereles, who went as far as to consider staying in Buenos Aires to confront Silva along with all the other stoolies who spied on behalf of the armed police. Malito imposed a degree of calm: now, more than ever, they had to use their intelligence and not allow themselves to be provoked.

Silva had picked up Fontán Reyes in the Esmeralda, a bar on Carlos Pellegrini Street, much frequented by tango players. The bar was close to the SADAIC* and you could always spot the young rising stars and the old fading ones, now retired

---

* Society of Musical Composers, also a coffee-house and meeting-place.

from the world of entertainment. When Silva came in with his own armed gang, everyone in the place froze, as if immobilized inside a bell jar. That was the sensation he produced every time he went into a dive like this. Silence, slow motion, expressions of fear.

Fontán Reyes was an elegant sort, despite carrying a number of excess kilos and the lit-up look of a drug addict. Silva approached and sat down beside him.

'You seem to be nervous. That's logical. Everyone turns nervous when I approach to speak to them,' said the commissioner.

This was the way (according to the papers) he could figure out how the robbery on the Town Hall was planned. The lead came from the Executive Committee, via Councillor Carlos A. Nocito, thirty-five years of age, married, the fraternal cousin of Atir Omar Nocito, alias Fontán Reyes, employed as a Public Works inspector in the San Fernando district. He was a man of influence, someone given to granting favours in the borough, a typical example of a local politician who flirted on the brink of illegal activity. In another situation, he would have been a *mafioso*, but here he dedicated himself to petty business deals: bribery and protection rackets; the illegal lottery; underworld brothels. He was a member of a gambling den in Olivos, servicing their interests along various points of the coast, and was himself the son of don Máximo Nocito, alias Nino, president of the San Fernando Council Executive Committee, voted in by the Popular Unity party. Detained and interrogated, Nocito ended up finally admitting that he'd met with the 'ranchers' introduced to him by his cousin Fontán Reyes, and that he'd spoken to them regarding the assault on the district's wages officers. Their meetings were held in a luxury apartment on Arenales Street.

Blanquita Galeano, Mereles' little concubine, is (according to the papers) a young middle-class girl, raised in a decent home and with the respect of her neighbours in the district of Caseros. Until she was fifteen years old, her behaviour was normal, she went to local dances, occasionally to her friends' houses, but that summer she'd decided to take off alone to Mar del Plata. Blonde and lanky, pretty and well-dressed, her figure had apparently impressed the son of a landowner who was living it up in the happy city. His name was Carlos Alberto Mereles. Expensive colour photos bore witness to their burgeoning romance. Then to its reversals. How long did it take Blanca to realize that Mereles was a criminal? One month, maybe two? It was already too late when she did so. At the end of August they got married. Or at least, she believed they did. Now the police have discovered that their marriage certificate was falsified and the ceremony itself a farce. Blanquita, the little sixteen-year-old girl, is currently in the hands of the Martínez Bureau of Investigations.

The Girl finally confessed that Mereles and three accomplices had abandoned the flat on Arenales Street a few hours before the police arrived, and took with them the larger part of the money from the raid along with the heavy weaponry, but she could (or would) not reveal the gunmen's present whereabouts. According to statements given by the youngster, the criminals had to be nearby, everyone went in fear of them, no one would offer them assistance and Malito, the gangsters' leader, had decided to chance it.

'He headed off to Tigre,' said the Girl, badly beaten by now, wiping the blood away with a handkerchief. 'There's a Polish guy out there going to help him. That's all I know.'

The Pole was Count Mitzky, who controlled the network of smugglers and petty thieves along the River Plate; he'd bought all the customs officers and those working for the Prefecture, now accustomed to turning a blind eye to the clandestine operations taking place between the two river-banks.

Silva ordered the Delta to be searched, going upriver as far as the edge of Isla Muerta, and then returned to the harbour bar where they'd found Twisty Bazán's body. No traces remained: Malito was two hours ahead of him.

When consulted by the press, the owners of the bistro at number 3300 Arenales Street* said it was a daily surprise to observe what the people opposite were purchasing at all hours of the day and night. Whole suckling pigs, rows of chickens on a spit, quantities of bottles of the finest wine. Thousands of pesos every day, and they always paid cash on the nail. The neighbour claimed that it was a matter of certain 'cattle owners' with business interests down in Patagonia and estates in the Venado Tuerto region. The proprietor of an important musical equipment store on Santa Fe Avenue like-wise insisted as much. Two gentlemen who used to live at 3300 Arenales Street had made an extremely large purchase a few months earlier. Tape recorders, portable radios, stereo players, a complete discotheque. The sheer quantity and value of what they'd bought required the shopkeeper's per-sonal attention. So he went along to supervise the installation

---

* i.e. 3.3 kilometres out of town.

of these valuables in 'the most luxurious apartment you ever saw', as he later confirmed to the journalists.

'You could see they were people with money, highly educated, with refined habits, and it was my belief that they'd come from the capital specifically to attend the polo championships on the fields at Palermo.'

Two days after the robbery the authorities had revealed details of the raid. Although those who had conducted it were now fugitives, the police had detained seven accomplices and informers, including a Town Hall employee, a well-known tango singer, the son and a nephew of the president in the local San Fernando Council, and a minor army officer, a middleman who had sold on the arms used by the criminals. This was the epilogue to an unheard-of occurrence, in which seemingly honest individuals hired assassins on to the payroll to commit a barbaric act of pillage.

Within the best-informed circles, the impression was deliberately given that the police were convinced the Argentine criminals had already succeeded in crossing over to Uruguay.

'Those who fled' (said Commissioner Silva, speaking off the record) 'are dangerous individuals, antisocial elements, homosexuals and drug addicts,' to which the Chief of Police added, 'They're not out of Tacuara, nor are they from the Peronist resistance, they're common criminals, psychopaths and murderers with extensive police records.'

'Hubris' was a word the youngster who wrote up the police reports in *El Mundo* was busily checking in the dictionary. It was defined as 'the arrogance of one who defies the gods and brings about their own downfall'. He decided to ask whether he could use such a title for a strapline in the paper and began writing his copy.

The one responsible for eliminating the prisoners in cold blood during the bank raid was Franco Brignone, alias the Kid, alias Angel Face, firstborn son of a wealthy entrepreneur in the construction business, resident of the rich suburb of Belgrano, who began his criminal way of life in 1961 at the age of seventeen, when he was a secondary school pupil at St George's, a smart English boarding-school, and was imprisoned for being the accomplice in an attempted robbery which ended up as a case of homicide. He was the favourite son of a respectable businessman, who'd enjoyed unlimited indulgence in being permitted to grow up dominating both his father's will and that of his younger siblings. One night he took the car and went in search of some friends – those he'd got to know at the Excursionistas Football Club – who'd ask him to go out and collect musical equipment. Waiting at the wheel, not getting out of the car, Brignone wasted hours, only for his friends to finally return empty-handed. His mates then explained that they'd fallen out with the bar owner and he'd refused to lend them any of the gear. The following day, the young man – still a minor – read in the paper that right there in the bar a man had been killed in the course of a robbery. He'd been beaten to death with a crowbar, one which just happened to be permanently stored underneath the Kid's car seat. The youngster went off to jail for the first time. The shock to his father was so severe that he died of a heart attack when he heard the news. The judge told Brignone that while the sentence might have been for mere complicity, he deserved to go down for parricide.

When he came out of jail, despite the money he inherited from his father and his mother's and brothers' desperation –

they being respected and honest members of the professional classes – but under the influence of his prison contacts, he embarked on a path of crime.

'In clink' (he would sometimes recount) 'I learnt what life is: you're inside and they bug you, and you soon learn to lie and to swallow the venom inside you. It was in jail I turned into a rent-boy, a drug addict, I became a real thief, a Peronist, and a card sharp; I learnt to fight dirty, how to use a headbutt to split the nose of anyone who tried to split your soul from your body if you so much as looked at them the wrong way; how to carry a joint hidden in my balls, and to stash the wraps of dope in my arsehole; I read every history book in the library, I didn't know what else to do with myself, you can ask me who won which battle in whatever year you choose and I'll tell you, 'cause in jail you have fuck-all to do and so you read, gaze into space, you get annoyed by the noise made by the brutes they bang up there, you become poisoned and you fill up with venom – you might as well have inhaled the stuff; you listen to the cons forever repeating the same nonsense, you think it must be Thursday by now but it's really still only coming up to Monday afternoon; I learnt to play chess, how to make belts out of silver foil from cigarette packets I stuck together; how to fuck my girlfriend when we were allowed together in the yard during visiting hour, in a kind of small tent made out of a sheet, over to one side. The other prisoners helped you out, if they were also at it with their wives and the kids were there too and they needed to hide to get it off, those whores are made of steel, they pull down their knickers and get astride you, while the screws look on, they really enjoy it, laughing at how dumb and hot you are for them, grown men with no chance to make it, because that's why you're banged up, to stop you fucking, and that's why you fill up with poison, they've got you in an ice box, they put you in a cage full of males and none of you can fuck, you want to and they beat you, or worse, they make you feel like a beggar, a hobo, you end up talking to yourself, hallucinating' (and the Gaucho let him ramble on, saying yes every so often, sometimes going so far as to take his hand, in the darkness, both of them awake, smoking, face upwards, in bed, in some room, in some hotel, in some provincial village, hidden, on guard, two twins hand in hand, slagging off the cops, with the pistol wrapped in a towel on the floor beside them, the car concealed beneath the trees, taking a break, attempting to take a rest and calm down, to leave off going wild for one night at least, and get to sleep in a bed).

And the Kid wouldn't let up, it was there he'd learnt to feel the screws' venom when they bugged him, just because . . . because he was young, because he was pretty, because your cock was bigger than theirs (said the Kid), 'I learnt to store all the hatred inside, that terrible poison, like a fire, loathing is what keeps you alive, you spend the night unable to sleep, in the cage, staring at the lightbulb on the ceiling, swinging away feebly, half yellow, lit up twenty-four hours a day so that they can always spy on you, forcing you to keep your hands outside the bedcovers, so you can't have a wank, and when a screw goes by and looks in through the spyhole, he sees you there, awake and thinking. Above all you learn to think in the clink: by definition a prisoner is a guy who spends the day thinking. D'you remember, Gaucho? You live inside your head, you withdraw inside it, invent yourself another life, right inside your brain, you come and go inside your mind, as though it were a screen, as if you had your own

personal television set, you have your very own channel and
project your life on it, the life you could be leading, isn't that
right, little brother? You turn to rubber, and you go deep
inside and travel, with whatever quantity of drug you can
muster, bye-bye, you're off, taking a taxi, getting down at the
street corner where your old woman lives, going into the bar
at the crossroads of Rivadavia and Medrano Streets, to look
out of the window at the fellows sweeping the pavement, or
at whatever takes your fancy. On one occasion I spent three
days building a house, I swear, beginning with the founda-
tions and then building upwards, working by memory, the
structure, the joints, every floor and wall, the staircase, the
roof, all the furniture and soft furnishings. Once you've finished building, you set a bomb and blow it all up, 'cause the
whole time you're there thinking that everyone is trying to
drive you mad. That's what they're there for. And, sooner or
later, they do drive you mad. That's if you spend the whole
time thinking. At the end of the day you've had so many
thoughts and so little movement that you are, I dunno, like
those fellows who go off and climb a mountain and sit themselves down to meditate for six or seven years, right? Hermits,
they used to call them, off in a cave, those guys, thinking
about God, the Holy Virgin Mary, making vows, refusing to
eat, just like you, really, when you're inside, so many thoughts
and so little actual experience, you end up like a skull, like a
flower-pot growing a plant, those thoughts are devouring you
like worms in dung. If I told you everything I thought when
I was inside I'd have to keep talking, I dunno, probably for the
same amount of time I was a prisoner. I'd remember little
girls of eight or ten years old I'd known at school, and I'd see
them grow up, I'd see them develop, filling out, and at siesta

time I'd watch their skinny legs in their little white ankle socks, their little tits starting to stick out, and within a week of being in that state I was already getting them moving, I didn't allow them to grow up too much. And I'd take and shove them down on to the embankment, 'cause alongside the traintrack there's some wasteland, there before you get to the canefields and a short strip of countryside, and it was there I went and shagged them, making them lie on their backs, holding them face upwards too, both my hands under their butt, then I pushed it into them, well all this thinking took about an hour, and in the end I took their virginity. In fact there was one who went to school with me, it must have been in about third grade, and afterwards I began to think I'd really taken her to the embankment at Adrogué where the train goes around the bend towards Burzaco. This girl wanted to be a virgin on her wedding night because her fiancé was a doctor, you know, someone with plenty of money, and so I took her the other way. I told her, your hubby won't notice anything, you'll stay sealed and intact, and she lay there face down in the field, with my cock stuck in her arse, a young girl aged fifteen, maximum, a real little whore, placid as could be because she was going to her wedding with an unruptured hymen, all very medical. Sometimes I'd think of a woman and I'd sense her there on the cell windowsill and I'd begin sucking her clitoris, she could be any kind of girl, my sister if you like. But the women aren't the worst of it because, for good or ill, you can see the women, the worst part is being banged up so you can't live, it's as if you were dead, and you have to do what they want, and that whole empty life breaks you apart in the end, it fills you with resentment and with venom. That's why whoever goes to prison is jail-meat, goes in and out, in and out, and that's because of the well of poison they fill you up with.'

The Kid had sworn that they would never get him inside again, they'd have to catch him asleep, but even then they'd never get him, and not even asleep could they carry him inside. For the time being he was protected, in the safehouse, down in the centre of Montevideo, but he couldn't just stay placidly indoors, there too he felt banged up, having to wait, always having to wait, staring at Malito and at Mereles and at the two Uruguayan fixers, playing poker for hours, not being able to tolerate the quiet, the lock-up, he wanted to get out and take a breather. The Gaucho whiled away the hours asleep, he'd come across another stash, opium, morphine, who knows what, he was always turning over chemists' shops or finding mules who'd bring him pills, drops, crystals, whatever, and he lived in the clouds, those early days after they arrived in Montevideo, stretched out on a bed, harmonizing (as Mereles would have it) with the voices of his madness.

By contrast Kid Brignone couldn't remain quiet, he was filled with foreboding, the need to breathe fresh air, and so he went out for a walk once twilight fell. He was convinced that if the police were on the warpath, it didn't matter what they did, and if the police weren't on the warpath, the chances of encountering them were remote. Malito let him get on with it. There was a degree of fatalism in each one of them and no one could imagine the turn that events would take.

Those who live under pressure, in situations of extreme danger, persecuted and accused, know that chance is far more important than courage in order to survive in combat. But this wasn't a fight, more a complex movement of dilatory manoeuvres, of waiting and procrastination. They were hoping the storm would end, they'd reach calm, and Nando would send a courier to get them overland into Brazil.

The Kid began to pace the old city, along the main drags of Sarandí and Colón Streets. He liked Montevideo, it was a tranquil city, of little low houses. He was weary of waiting so he regularly left the house at nightfall. The Gaucho watched him leave, knowing where he was going, without asking questions, without saying anything. He'd made himself a kind of lair in the corner, in a gap in the stairwell, the Gaucho, and he lay down there to dream about, or to sketch the cars he found in *Popular Mechanics*. The Kid invited him to come out a couple of times, but the Gaucho didn't want to know. 'I'm staying right here, in my filthy pad,' he said with a smile, wearing his Clipper sunglasses which gave him (or so he thought) the look of an aviator, a man of the world, living forever in twilight, in penumbra, isolated in his refuge. Then the Kid would salute him and leave, setting off down the street with a sense of adventure, on meeting the scent of the coast, the sour stench coming up from the port.

Mingling with the gangsters and queers taking a walk around Montevideo's Plaza Zavala there are always some lost girls. They're all youngsters, though generally prematurely hardened. They know everything about the lads they do it with, and with whom they sometimes live: that the boys seek out others and either pay or charge them. Despite knowing all this, they don't care. From time to time one of the girls goes to the park with her stooge and they sit there together until he picks up a punter and they separate as if by tacit accord: the lad goes off with his trick, and the girl goes off to the corner café to wait for him.

One of the girls aroused the Kid's curiosity. She was the

most arresting to look at: she must have been about nineteen, with long black hair and hypnotic eyes. She watched the men with a kind of smile that gave her a pensive air, as if to her the world, while miserable and corrupt, amused and filled her with the will to live. There was something special about this girl, as if she were in some way absent, as if she regarded everything from a great distance.

Just outside the park the police had picked up a lad dressed like a queen, his face thick with make-up, wearing a blond wig. The girl smiled and commented: 'Another Queen of the Night taken prisoner for disobeying the rules of trade.'

The Kid abandoned his seat and went to sit beside the girl, where they talked freely for a while. They left the café, then, and went into the park where they again sat down, opposite an old man who was preaching from a Bible propped on a lectern, with a microphone held to his lips.

'Christ's words are within us all, brothers and sisters.'

He spoke as if he were alone, the old man. And he gave a blessing, making the sign of the Cross in the air with his hand. He was wearing a dark frock-coat, and looked very dignified, like a priest perhaps, a little barmy, or perhaps a reformed alcoholic, escaped from the Salvation Army, a repentant sinner.

'Jesus was denied twice over and twice over the traitor was punished.'

The voice of the old man preaching mingled with the murmuring of the wind in the trees. For the first time in many months the Kid felt at ease and at peace. (For the first time, perhaps, since he'd joined Malito's gang, he felt safe.) There he was, sitting in the park with a girl, and he was pleased to be seen with her by some of the men who'd already been his tricks, guys who'd previously gone with him, last night or maybe the night before, in the toilets at the Rex cinema.

Suddenly she was looking at him with that smile of hers, surprising him when she said: 'There's something about you I find disconcerting. I've seen you in the cinema, and I've seen you scoring off the men here, and you seem just like the rest of them, but you're not, there's something different about you. You're more of a man . . .'

The girl said exactly what she thought, right out, and with total sincerity. The Kid was so used to faking it and everyone lying to him, that he took fright, felt really scared. He didn't like women who confronted him, or who told him he was a rent-boy.

'Lady,' he said. 'You seem a little confused to me. You talk all the time, chatter like a Uruguayan hen. Or are you a cop? A proper cop?' and the Kid laughed out loud. 'Are you a WPC from the Pocitos Division, by any chance? Or are you on the pull?'

She stroked his face and drew him closer.

'Quiet, now. Come, now, what are you on about, ssh . . . I only meant to say that I've kept my eye on you since you first turned up here, last Friday, with that velvet jacket of yours.' She took him by the arm, feeling the electric current and the softness of the fabric on the palm of her hand. 'And I can see who you are, and that you're not the same as the rest of them, you don't talk to anyone. And you're Argentine. You must be from Buenos Aires, aren't you?'

He was from Buenos Aires and lived in Buenos Aires, and had come to Montevideo on business, selling contraband fabrics. Whatever version you like, as long as it was believable, long enough to last until the next morning. All the Argentines

loose in Montevideo were smugglers. She smiled and then
laughed, looking even younger, and kissed him on the mouth
and then at once (just as the Kid had feared) began telling or
inventing her own story (like him).

She was working shifts in a night-club and came from
across the River Negro. She wanted to save money and invest
it in something for herself, in another part of the city, possibly
near Mercado, where there were some decent bars, an area the
queers didn't frequent, or any lowlife, none of the cheap
negroes who came down from the slums on the Cerro. She
liked Argentines because they were educated and because
they had a distinguished accent. She, in her turn, had a very
archaic manner of speaking, because she came from the interior, and because she said whatever came into her head.
She was genuine. Or she seemed genuine, perhaps a little
affected, but naturally so, as if she were a lady from an earlier
epoch (as though she was playing at what that sort of lady
might be like). Didn't he remember the outfits he saw as a
child in the pages of the Billiken magazine? For sure she did,
and she reeled off the titles: 'The Lion of France'; 'The
Dutchwoman'; 'The Old Lady'. The youngster was a simple
country girl, but she gave herself an air of grandeur, something at once authentic and theatrical, and which pleased
him. The girl could have been a sister to him and, at one and
the same time, a lost woman. He'd always wanted to have a
sister, a young and beautiful woman, in whom he could con-
fide and whom he would have been obliged to keep his body
well away from. A woman his own age, lovely to see, with
whom he'd be proud to be seen, without anyone needing to
know she was his sister. He felt as much, and after a little
while, told her as much, straight out.

'Your sister, you'd like me to be your sister?' the girl smiled in surprise, and the Kid roughly replied: 'Why? What's so funny about that?'

Like every guy who plays the man's role with their male partners (the girl was to explain later), the Kid was very touchy on the question of his masculinity.

The Kid was utterly fed up of going with bum boys. Every so often he got sick of it. At present he didn't want a single one of those boys circling the square to look at him, he'd known them under other circumstances, in a fleeting meeting, in toilets that stank of disinfectant, where monstrous acts were described and phrases of love were inscribed on the walls. There names were written up as if names of the gods, hearts were drawn with inartistic ardour, gigantic organs, depicted like sacred birds along the walls of the urinals in the stations and on the flip-up seats in the El Hindú cinema and in the cloakrooms of numerous clubs. He would suddenly feel the urge to humiliate himself, it came on like a sickness, or like grace descending, a breath in his heart, something you have no way of preventing. The same blind force which draws the person who experiences an irresistible desire to enter a church and make a confession. He would kneel in front of these unknown guys, bowing down (it would be better to say, or maybe he'd actually said so, added the girl) before them as though they were gods, knowing the whole time that the least false move, the faintest insinuation of a smile, of a joke, could lead him to kill them, that a mere false gesture was sufficient, one word too many, for them to die with an expression of shock and horror on their faces and a knife buried in their stomachs. They who stripped off their clothes, stock still like kings

before him, had no idea of who he was, they never imagined, they were incapable of intuiting the risk they were
running. The Kid might be powerful but he was kneeling
there on the ground, nauseous from the smell of disinfectant, while some unknown pervert talked to him then paid
him. Or was it he who paid? He could never clearly recall
what he'd done the previous night, nor the night before
last, during his escapades in the harbour bars and his pick-
ups in the El Hindú cinema. He could only recall the
irresistible pull that got him to his feet and out on to the
street, it was like a euphoria, that left him incapable of
thought (he told the girl, according to her later declaration), left him without any thoughts at all, vacant and free,
tied to one idea alone. It's like looking for something under
a white light and in the middle of the road. It's irresistible.
Until afterwards, somewhat disoriented, as if emerging from
a dream, he went back to the flat where Malito was waiting
for him, and where everyone was waiting for Nando to help
them across to Brazil, and whenever he arrived there the
Gaucho was huddled in silent withdrawal, maybe he was
furious, locked in what he called his 'filthy pad', in a corner,
upstairs, at the top of the stairwell. But she didn't pass on
any of this information (it was the Gaucho who did)
because the girl thought the Kid was a smuggler who traf-
ficked in English cashmere, who lived off the anthill that
controlled contraband manufacturing, and who had his
vices, like all the guys the girl had ever met since she came
to the city.

But the Kid, in contrast (and he himself said as much), felt
sane and safe with this girl, as if there were no possible danger
in being around her, he only had to let himself be carried

along by her for a while, far from the Blond Gaucho, the twin, and well away from the Crow, just for a while, like a normal sort of guy.

Meanwhile destiny had begun preparing its drama, weaving its intrigue, knotting off the last piece of wool (this was the youth's description when he wrote up the crime page for *El Mundo*), tying up all the loose threads of what those ancient Greeks were talking about when they said *muthos*.

'I've got a place near here. Some of the boys in the cabaret lend it to me, and they're never around,' she told him.

The flat had two bedrooms and a lounge and was in utter chaos: unwashed dishes piled high in the kitchen, leftover dope and food dropped on the floor, the girl's clothes hanging out of an open suitcase. There were two beds in one room, and a sofa and a mattress lying on a board on the floor of the other.

'A woman comes and cleans, but only on Mondays.'

'Who uses the place? It's a tip,' said the Kid.

'It belongs to some friends from the club where I work, I've already told you that. They let me use it during the week and on Saturday nights I go back to the hostel.'

The Kid took a turn around the pad, looked through the windows that gave on to an inner courtyard, at the passage that gave on to a staircase.

'And upstairs, what's there?'

'Another apartment and a flat roof.' She searched behind the bed and came out with a 45 r.p.m. record. 'Do you happen to like Head and Body . . .'

'What are you, telepathic? . . . Of course I like them, better than the Rolling . . .'

'That's it,' she said. 'They're fab, brilliant.'

'When I was a child I was clairvoyant,' the Kid chuckled to himself. 'But I had a problem and it cost me my psychic power.'

She looked at him, amused, convinced the guy was having her on.

'An accident?'

'Well, not me exactly, some friends who were travelling with me in the car began to mess about. We were all drunk – I used to drink gin in those days . . . I ended up inside. And I stopped seeing what I'd seen as a child.'

'Drinking is rough, I prefer hash,' the girl replied and perched on the arm of a chair to roll a marijuana joint. She looked like a hippie, the Kid suddenly noticed. A Uruguayan hippie, with those long clothes and her little pigtails, and she also worked in a cabaret, that was too much.

'For example, as a boy I saw my Uncle Federico who'd died two years earlier and talked to him too.'

She looked seriously and attentively at him, preparing the joint with deft movements. He told her the story when they began to smoke, because it was like talking about a period of life he'd lost, he'd never spoken to anybody when he was young, from the earliest times to the dead times in which he'd begun repeatedly getting locked up.

'My Uncle Federico was a great guy, who went under two or three times, but he always came up again ahead. He lived in Tandil, and I'd go and visit and stay over with him. He had a garage, and he fixed Kaiser cars, he did well out of it, but then one afternoon his son was struck by an explosion in the fusion welding, a really stupid accident, as there was an exposed cable which short-circuited, and my uncle ended up watching his son die. From that moment on, my uncle let himself go, didn't want to see anyone, spent the entire day stretched out on his bed with the Venetian blinds down, smoking and drinking *mate** and pondering. He emptied out his *mate* on to some newspapers in the flat, and in the end there was a sort of green island of dried herbs in the middle of the bedroom, and he wouldn't let anyone come in, not even to open the curtains,' or so the Kid related, according to the girl some time later, 'and just kept saying that he'd get up the next day. I went to visit him one afternoon and he was still there, lying in bed with his face to the wall, without doing anything. "Hi, Kid, how're you doing, when did you get here?" he said, as usual. Then he stayed silent for a while. "I've no great wish to get up," he said. "Do me a favour, buy me a pack of Particulares Fuertes." And when I got to the door he called me back. "Kid," he said, "better still, buy me two packs, then I'll have some in stock."

'That was the last time I saw Uncle Federico alive,' said the Kid and took a long, deep drag of his spliff and smelt the acrid smoke, first in his throat and then at the bottom of his lungs, 'because he died within the week, and from then on he began appearing to me with monotonous regularity.' He gave a belly laugh, as though he'd cracked a particularly funny joke. He couldn't stop giggling and the girl started to join in while they passed the joint back and forth. 'It was really weird, because he was dead, and I could see him plainly, stood there in front of me, knowing he was dead, but this didn't seem to matter at all. At this time I must have been

---

* *Mate* is a typically gaucho drink, traditionally drunk from a gourd through a silver straw, at intervals through the working day.

more or less the same age as Cholito when he died, some sixteen or seventeen years old, so that was why he appeared to me, no doubt, as if I were his son. If I came up close, say at a distance from here to the wall (when I saw him of course I knew it was a hallucination, but I saw him just as well as I'm seeing you), he'd be smoking a cigarette, and saying nothing to me. He smiled. Even when I spoke to him, he didn't hear, he just stayed put, smoking, partly hunched over, the ash forever on the point of dropping off the end of his cigarette. All he did was smile.' He suddenly started laughing, the Kid did, realizing how much he'd related to the girl. 'It was a ghost . . . And it appeared to me. I've never told anyone, but it's the truth.'

'I know,' she said, handing him the spliff. 'That's what I meant when I said there was something about you I found disconcerting. I mean you look as if you come from around here, but your spirit comes from somewhere else . . .' Hash, because it turned out to be hash rather than marijuana, made her speak slowly, as though she chose each word very carefully. 'What are you doing on this side of the River?'

'I'm passing through. On my way to Mexico . . . I've a friend living in Guanajuato . . . Poor thing . . .' he said, with nobody particular in mind. Could he be thinking of the Uruguayan girl or of his friend, the Queen, who'd gone to live in Guanajuato because he was sick of living in the capital? He'd also been thinking of his mother, of course, she was a poor thing, who by now must be aware that he was being hunted by the police, along with the rest of the world. 'My mother wanted me to study architecture. She wanted to have a son who created houses, because my dad ran a construction business.'

Smoking made him melancholy, it was always the same, it made him sad and made him relax, both at the same time, he felt slow and lucid.

'Me too, I'm passing through . . . I left home. Wait, I'd almost forgotten,' said the girl and quickly held out to him the butt of her joint clamped in a pair of eyebrow tweezers, then fell to her knees and started rummaging under the bed.

From somewhere way underneath she pulled out a Winco player and put a record on the turntable. It was a record with two sides by Head and Body (the tunes were 'Parallel Lives' and 'Brave Captain' and the girl had been listening to them for months on end, the entire time, without letting up, always the same, first one and then the other side until they'd both become scratched).

'Shall we play it?'

'Of course . . .' said the Kid.

'It's the only record I have,' said the girl.

'Parallel Lives' began playing at full blast, and they moved their bodies to the rhythm and smoked the marijuana spliff down so low they burned their lips on the butt. They could hear the throbbing music through the cheap record-player, it vibrated just as obsessively, and the two began to chorus in English along with the rock and roll.

*I spent all my money in a Mexican whorehouse*
*Across the street from a Catholic church.*
*And if I can find a book of matches*
*I'm goin' to burn this hotel down . . .*

He and the girl sang along together, in descant, in a rough

sort of English, copying the phonetics of the music with alternately merry and angry yelps.

When the record finished, the Kid sat down on the rumpled bed beside her and took her hand (which was very cold) and pressed it to himself with a sensation of strangeness and loss. Then he closed his eyes.

'Kid,' she said, speaking in a muddled manner but with great emotion, as though she were uttering profound truths. 'I know the scene only too well. You need to pretend that nothing matters to you at all and carry on in there with all those to whom nothing really does matter at all, or you'll drown in it all.'

He looked at her, waiting for what was to come, and she propped herself on one elbow and then, after a long pause, kissed him on the mouth. The girl had a confused and passionate way of speaking which he liked, as if she wanted to give the impression of being more serious and intellectual than she was, using words he couldn't follow at all.

'You're searching for something unknown and so you end up falling into despair,' she said and then hummed the next tune ('Brave Captain') by Head and Body which rang out forcefully, like a harder and fiercer version of the life they were leading.

*You got to tell me, brave captain,* she sang. *Why are the wicked so strong . . .*

'Take off your blouse.'

With a sudden start she realized the Kid was beginning to undress her, she stood up and began to feel offended.

'All you lot are always saying how macho you are and you take time out and do it with girls to prove it, but when you do it with each other, you always say it's only for money. Why don't you give it up, if you really want to leave off and flee into your own inner world so much? Give it a miss for now. Go find a job.'

'I work the whole time and I don't want to be talking about this kind of crap,' he answered, on the defensive.

'But you always go back to it. Do you do it with machos? Do you like it that way round?'

She was sincere and ruthless. He nodded slowly and seriously.

'Yes . . .'

'Since when?'

'I dunno. What does it matter?'

She hugged him and he, almost without thinking, went on talking, as if he were alone. The girl then began to grind the hash into a delicate little pipe with a round bowl, where the drug burned and crackled.

It was a disease, this going out at night like a vagabond, seeking out humiliation and pleasure.

'I'm bored,' said the Kid. 'Aren't you bored? I like men, from time to time, 'cause when I've spent a long while without going out, I get bored. I'm married and my wife is a teacher, we live in a house in Liniers, and I've two sons.' Lying helped him to speak and he could see the girl's face illuminated by the glow of the drug and then he felt the warmth of the pipe in his hand and the smoke going down into his lungs and he felt passably happy. 'But family life doesn't interest me. My wife is a saint, and my children are real little pigs. I only get along with my brother, I've a twin brother. Non-identical. Did I tell you about him? They call him the Gaucho, because he lived in the countryside for a long time, out in Dolores . . . He has a nervous disorder, he's extremely quiet and hears voices talking to him. I look after him, and care more about him than about my wife and sons. Is there anything wrong in that? Life' – it was hard work for him to connect his thoughts – 'life is like a freight train, haven't you watched one of them go by at night? It goes so slowly, you can't see the end, it seems it'll never finish going by, but finally you're left behind, watching the tiny red light on the back of the last carriage as it disappears into the distance.'

'Dead right,' she replied. 'Freight trains, crossing the countryside, in the night. Do you want more?' she asked him. 'I've got some. It's good, isn't it? Brazilian. When I was a child back in my village, I used to watch trains and there was always some old tramp taking a ride on the top. I'm from across the River Negro, the trains came up from the south and carried on all the way to Rio Grande do Sul.'

They remained peaceful, lying on their backs, in silence, for a long time. They heard a train go by every so often, and the Kid realized that the sound reminded him of the freight trains running through Belgrano when he was a boy. The girl began to undress him. The Kid turned round and began kissing her and stroking her breasts. She sat down on the bed and within an instant had stripped off her clothes. Her skin was white, it shone like a lamp in the twilight of the room.

'Wait,' she said, when he was on the point of entering her. She leapt, stark naked, from the bed. She went to the bathroom and returned with a condom. 'It's impossible to know where you guys have stuck your pricks,' she said brutally, as though she were a third party, as though up until then it had all been a game that was now over, and it was time to start behaving like a proper prostitute. He held her down by the wrists, flattened, and with her arms outstretched across the bed, murmuring to her as he kissed her neck.

'And you?' he asked, without letting her budge. 'Every last one of the guys down the Mercado clubs has had you . . . several times over.' He regretted the words as soon as they were out of his mouth.

'I know, I know,' she sighed regretfully.

Then they embraced with a kind of desperation and she said to him: 'I still haven't told you who I am. They call me Giselle but my name is Margarita.' She felt for his penis and inserted it between her raised legs. 'Go slowly,' she said, guiding him, 'give it me.'

They paused in between times to resume smoking and listening to Head and Body and in the end she turned around naked and supported herself on the windowsill, her buttocks lifted, her back towards him. The Kid slowly entered her until he could feel the girl's flanks against his stomach.

'Push hard inside me,' she said and twisted her face to kiss him.

He pressed against the nape of her neck, her hair short and rough, and she turned her face again with her eyes wide open and moaned loudly and afterwards spoke to him gently, in soft tones, as if she were apologizing, sighing again as she did so.

'Your prick will get covered in shit, your whole cock coated with shit.'

The Kid felt himself come and fell back.

He withdrew from her and wiped himself on the sheet. Then he turned over on to his back and lit a cigarette. The girl stroked his chest and he felt himself fall asleep for the first time, after months and months of relentless insomnia.

From that afternoon onwards, and during the whole of the

following week, he'd drop in frequently at the Mercado café and they'd stay in the empty flat together. They always played the same Head and Body record, always both sides, which they now knew by heart, and they'd smoke some hash and talk together until they fell asleep. He began leaving her money, which she accepted as completely natural.

A while ago, but not all that long ago (according to what the newspapers would later report), the country girl had come from the interior, her head filled with illusions about the capital city. She was from the other side of the River Negro, but the river waters cascading over the dam weren't the only mirror she needed to reflect her growing up. She came to Montevideo with the hope and candour typical of youthful feminine beauty. Once in the city, she became increasingly caught up in the shining threads of night life and of a club called the Bonanza, shortly before moving on to another called the Sayonara, to end up in another one in the centre, known as the Moulin Rouge, where she found a man friend who set her on course working as a high-class escort. This friend was one of the night-club owners.

It was through this very club that two farmers from the eastern region of the country came to sublet the flat from the night-club owner. The place itself was in the city centre, and the rent was kept low, while the flat contained everything necessary for a proper bachelor pad. But this friendship born of regular night-time contact soon turned the apartment into a place for the country girl to stay in: a favour* that the

---

* Expressed in the original as a *gauchada*, an ironic reference to the fact that *gauchos* can always be counted on to honour pledges – and defend their honour – and that of others, particularly vulnerable women.

new owners of the flat generously afforded the night-club owner.

Later on, as if by chance, the deal became more complicated and the flat generated an increasing number of keys which gave access to increasing numbers of casual users. The previous evening, for example, one of the waiters from the club had stayed there and had left behind all his documents, some personal possessions and a few clothes. The more regular occupants of the flat on the corner of Julio Herrera and Obes Streets turned a blind eye to its use for occasional nocturnal encounters. No reason to be surprised, then, at this chain of circumstances, for in this multiplication of actual and apparent tenants and of owners, you'd find the keys to the series of errors that terminated in bringing in the boys from Buenos Aires. So now it's out in the open: by the scanty light in the dingy corners of a cabaret strange friendships form, which have a tendency to evaporate in the clear light of day.

# 5

Miss Lucía noticed two men changing the licence plates on a Studebaker parked close to the corner and it seemed a little strange to her. One held a screwdriver, or perhaps it was only a penknife, she couldn't see too clearly at that distance, and was crouching to loosen the screws on the metal plate while the other, a big blond fellow with a bandage around his neck, held the new one in place. The woman slept in a shed on the patch of land at the back of the bakery and today had been awoken by the dawn light. She opened up the shop and had to put on the lights because it was still dark. From the window, whilst she sipped her *mate*, she became absorbed in watching the figures of the two men who, squatting next to one another, were cracking jokes and larking about. Or that's what Lucía surmised, because never for an instant did she see them look either concerned or stealthy, or even apprehensive over being caught out. Rather, they seemed to be carrying out their project as easily as they might have changed a car tyre.

Lucía was very observant, her job in the bakery had developed her particular aptitude for observation, almost a sixth sense (she would later declare), because she had the ability to remember the face of the most casual customer if she happened on them in even the remotest city street, and several days later. But she needed no special powers of observation to understand what was happening on the corner with those guys fiddling about with the car plates on the Studebaker. Everyone knew each other in this district of Montevideo and it was highly exceptional for anything out of the ordinary to happen, for inexplicable occurrences to take place. In all the years she'd assumed a post in front of the shop, there'd only ever been one man who had had a car accident and he died on the pavement, all of a sudden and of a heart attack. He just lay there on the street, his mouth wide open, unable to breathe, and attempted to cover his face with a white handkerchief. Lucía approached when the man was already dead and stayed alone with the body in front of the bakery until the owner of the corner chemist's shop appeared and called an ambulance.

This time matters were different, and there was the chance to intervene before it got too late. That was why she lifted the receiver and vacillated, for she didn't like getting mixed up in other people's lives, but she experienced a weird emotion, as though an important matter had been entrusted into her hands, and called the police. As soon as she did so, she switched off the bakery light and remained stock still there, just staring out.

She again had the sensation she called 'the evil temptation', an impulse that sometimes caused her to be hurtful or to let someone else be hurtful to another, a temptation she had had to struggle against since her earliest childhood. For example, when the man had the heart attack, she remained silent, watching him die, and always thought that if she had reacted rather than allow herself to be swept along by the curiosity that had paralysed her, while the man with the livid face struggled and suffocated, spread eagled on the flagstones of the pavement, the man with the handkerchief over his face could have been saved. Now, in contrast, she acted almost without hesitation and, after lodging her complaint, settled herself to await the outcome. It looked like nothing more than a straightforward car heist, and she could never have envisaged what she was about to witness.

You could monitor the whole street, in this quiet district of Montevideo, just by looking through the plate glass window. 'Better than the cinema,' Miss Lucía Passero was to say later on.

A real orgy of blood (according to the papers) thus began in Uruguay on Wednesday, 4 November 1965, when from the bakery located on the corner of Enriqueta Comte and Riqué Streets, almost on Marmarajá Street, it was noted that on the opposite side of the road a red Studebaker was parked, inside which two men were sitting and smoking calmly.

Moments later a second vehicle appeared – a black Hillman – from which another couple of unknown men got out, and handed a package to the former arrivals. The Hillman departed with its occupants and stopped on the street corner. It could then be observed that the two men emerged from the Studebaker and gave themselves the task of setting about exchanging the licence plates for new ones contained in the package of which they had taken delivery a few seconds earlier.

Two policemen appeared at the corner and approached the Studebaker. The first person to catch sight of them in the mirror was Crow Mereles.

'It's the cops,' he said.

The Crow opened the car door and leaned on the mudguard, smoking, serene, as the two policemen approached. One was black, or rather half-caste, with flat features and tightly curled hair, and the other was a fat guy, exactly like every other fat cop in the city. There were lots of policemen who let themselves go and who got breathless if ever they ran, and whose only useful purpose was to kick the shit out of the poor sods who'd already been brought to the ground and were now lying there, defenceless, in the street; aiming their blows to the kidneys with the full weight of their enormous bodies behind them. But a negro – Crow had never seen a black cop. Or maybe they had them in Brazil. But then he'd never been to Brazil. And in North America, of course, the black cops in films from the United States used to kill other black North Americans all over the streets of the Bronx. That phrase formed in his head like a refrain while he allowed the two men to approach him. They were going to ask him for his documents. Mereles smiled amiably. The black was a couple of paces behind, and the fat guy approached them first.

'Leave him to me,' said Gaucho Dorda.

The fat policeman saluted him by tipping the front of his peaked cap with his index finger, and looked inside the car with a scowl. The Gaucho loathed pigs above all else, and before the guy had time to draw breath, he fired a shot into his chest. The man fell to the ground but did not die immediately, bawling, searching for cover under the edge of the kerb. The other policeman, the black, jumped out of the way, then crouched behind the car and began firing.

'Cancela,' the black told him, 'call Headquarters.'

Cancela must have had a walkie-talkie, but he was in no state to use it. He was lying in the gutter (Lucía could see him perfectly clearly), his chest stained with blood, breathing, or rather snoring – it sounded like – with difficulty, shifting his hand to cover the wound, to try, perhaps, to staunch the haemorrhage that was filling his throat with blood.

Dorda put his arm out of the Studebaker window and gave Cancela the *coup de grâce* in his stomach. Dorda laughed out loud.

'Die, pig,' he said and took aim at the other policeman while the Crow revved up the car and set it in motion.

But the black was brave and leapt forward firing with his .45 and the twins crouched down in the car because he'd succeeded in wounding the Uruguayan they were bringing with them.

The black paused in the middle of the street and continued firing while Mereles accelerated the car and set off around the corner with a squeal of tyres. During the exchange the black completely emptied his gun and had to take a moment's refuge on the threshold of the chemist's shop to reload. Following this (Lucía Passero continued) he went on firing until the car and its criminal occupants disappeared. It was like seeing a film projected for her alone, an unforgettable experience, those men crouched down and shooting, their faces frozen, their eyes steady, the dunglike smell of the gunpowder, the near-chestnut colour of the blood, the squeal of the tyres on the escaping car and the focused expression on the face of the black grasping his pistol in his two hands, holding steady, his legs spread wide on the paving stones. 'I saw,' said the woman, 'that one of the evil-doers had been wounded,' and it was true, she saw exactly how a bullet smashed the car's rear window as it passed by the bakery and saw also how one of those men shook his head and kept touching his waist, each time staring at the blood on his hand as he lifted it.

'They got me,' the Uruguayan said and lowered his head to look at his blood-soaked hands as he pressed them against his abdomen. He was calm and frantic at one and the same time, so surprised at what had happened to him, he didn't know how to react. He was called Yamandú Raymond Acevedo and had never been wounded before. He'd agreed to work with the Argentines on the car job because they were paying him a load of money and had promised him more to take them to the Brazilian frontier, to Rio Grande do Sul, up north past Santa Ana.

'We can't keep going with you,' Kid Brignone was calmly saying to his face. 'Sorry, brother, but you'll have to get out.'

'You're sending me to my death, Kid, don't leave me here in this state, I beg you, for God's sake.'

Yamandú looked at him, whey-faced, begging first the Kid and then Dorda, who had the Beretta resting across his knees.

'You're fucked, Yamandú,' said the Gaucho, 'you'll have to sort yourself out alone, we have to keep on going, nothing's going to happen to you.'

'Don't be a bastard, Argie, don't just hand me over, let's go to Malito's and let him decide what to do.'

Dorda lifted his Beretta and pointed it at his temple. 'Be grateful that I'm not polishing you off. If you get caught and sing, be sure I'll find you and cut off your balls.'

'You're a pile of shit, you lot, you can't treat people like this,' replied the Uruguayan.

The Crow barely slowed down and Yamandú opened the car door. He was going to have to chuck himself out in order to avoid being killed. He threw himself as far as possible from the car and fell sideways on to the tarmac.

The car accelerated again and Dorda stuck the gun out of the window and fired at him, without managing to score a direct hit. To Yamandú this was proof that the Argentines were a lost cause, because there was an unwritten law in operation, a code of honour that you had to respect. Nobody abandons a wounded comrade who has behaved with absolute loyalty as if he were a nark. 'They were mad killers,' said Yamandú, 'living in complete delirium, they wanted to reach New York by car along the PanAmerican Highway, raiding banks along the way and robbing pharmacies for drug supplies. They were obsessed with this, they studied maps of all the side roads, and calculated how long it would take to get to North America. They were off their heads, hallucinating that they'd be working for the Puerto Rican mafia in New York, getting into the 'hood, into the Latin ghetto and starting over there, where nobody knew them. They couldn't even get out of Montevideo city centre, and they wanted to get to New York because the Kid had heard the tango singer who set up the robbery for them saying he'd met a Cuban with a restaurant in New York and they wanted to go and get into business with him, crazy stuff like that. I have never,' added Yamandú, 'come across guys like these.' No doubt Yamandú exaggerated, in order to shift the immense pressure he felt he was under and make himself out to be a simple bumpkin, no more than a stool-pigeon of the Argentines, who forced him to get involved in things he would never otherwise have gone near.

'He'll squeal,' said the Gaucho, enraged at not having succeeded in finishing him off. 'He'll bring the lot of us down with him . . . He knows all the houses, hiding places, where the hell are we going to go now?'

'Calm down and let me think,' replied the Kid.

'Think, what can you think about? That animal will squeal, fucking creep that he is, we have to go back and waste him.'

'He's right,' said the Crow and reversed and then swung round at full speed, the car returning to the avenue where they'd dumped the Uruguayan. But when they got there, Yamandú had succeeded in dragging himself across a plot of wasteland and was hiding there, in a shed on the yard at the back of the hairdresser's, waiting for nightfall and the chance to make his getaway. He also persuaded himself, hidden there in a kind of covered gallery where the dryers were stored, looking like scuba-diving helmets with metal feet, the revolving armchairs with their white leather armrests, the basins with their round bowls pushing forward and all the tubes and sprays for hair-washing behind, with mirrors and boxes of combs and curlers, that he could just about hear the engine of the car that had returned and was searching the streets for him and it also seemed to him he could hear (or imagined he could hear) the Gaucho's voice calling him as if he were a kitten: 'Pussy, pussy, pussy.' 'He was entirely capable of doing that' (according to Yamandú) 'for he was a total speedfreak, completely off his head, who did whatever the Kid ordered him to, and the Kid was colder than a snake, he didn't care nothing for no one.'

They took several turns around the area and even passed the plot of wasteland and the shed where Yamandú was hidden, but they didn't manage to find him and so left the centre when they heard the sound of approaching police patrol sirens. Without a doubt the police now had the details on the car, and as soon as he fell into their hands the Uruguayan would provide them with all the information necessary to identify them. As ever, Malito was off by himself, on his own in a pad over on Pocitos unknown to anyone, setting up a connection to get him back into Buenos Aires should the crossing into Brazil go awry. They had an appointment to meet him the following day. But by then he would already be aware of what had been happening.

'We need to get clear altogether,' said the Crow. 'Fall back and regroup.'

'Let's go, then,' said the Kid. 'Let's try and get there ahead of the cops.'

They were absolutely certain that Yamandú was about to fall into their hands and that, of course, he'd see them stuffed. They stopped off at the safehouse where they'd been holed up since coming to Montevideo, and grabbed their arms and the money five minutes before the police got there. From then onwards, they broke all contact with the network Nando had set up for them in Uruguay, and began looking for somewhere to hide. They were completely cut off, everyone shunned them as if they were lepers.

'I know where to go,' Kid Brignone said after a while.

'D'you have a pad?' asked the Crow.

They had paused in a side street off the main drag of the Rambla, facing the river. They had hidden the car under some trees in the Parque Rodo, and were tipping back beer from the bottle sitting on the running-board, with the car doors open, and the guns and cash stashed in the hole left by their removal of the rear passenger seats.

'Wait here, you lot.'

The Kid crossed the road, entered a café, and looked for a pay phone at the back of the bar.

By this time Yamandú had been discovered in the middle of a ladies' hairdresser. The police out patrolling the district found him crouched at the back of the shop. In spite of the wound in his abdomen, the gunman attempted to escape but was brought down. He begged for mercy on his knees and finally implicated all his associates, letting them know how he got connected.

'Don't kill me,' he pleaded, 'it was all the Argies' fault.'

Their subject before them was one Yamandú Raymond Acevedo, of Uruguayan nationality, and with a long police record. He was taken to the Military Hospital, where he received first aid. The doctors did their utmost to keep him awake and alert.

Raymond, under police interrogation, admitted to having been party to the gunfight in which police officer Cancela met his death, further admitting that he had continued on in the company of the Argentine criminals until they, in view of the fact that he – Yamandú – could no longer continue the flight because of his wound, attempted to kill him. His lengthy statement to the police allowed them to make a step-by-step reconstruction of their movements from the time they reached Montevideo. At the same time, the police immediately set in motion a series of raids to intercept the gang's progress.

Having gathered sufficient physical details and particular characteristics of the four, they made contact with the police force across the River (again, according to the press). Then a series of photographic portraits of the gunmen confirmed their Argentine nationality. Of the four men in the group, Yamandú recognized three of the Argentine assailants from the rogues' gallery. They were Mereles, Brignone and Dorda. However, he knew nothing of where one Enrique Mario Malito was holed up.

The criminal world found itself in a 'state of alert', for the investigations clearly demonstrated that the assassins, along with local swindlers and smugglers, had collaborated in concealing the Argentine gunmen, and were now in fear of police reprisals. The latest version to circulate was that Malito's gang had set off for Colonia in a desperate attempt to return across the River Plate into Buenos Aires. Today (or perhaps yesterday) the smuggler known as Omar Blasi Lentini had been detained, along with his pregnant wife and his two small children, for having procured shelter for the gang in the home of customs officer Pedro Glasser at number 2108 San Salvador Avenue. At once, the police were on the tracks of the Argentine criminal Hernando Heguilein, 'Nando', former member of the National Liberation Alliance (ALN) during Perón's reign, and accused by Lentini of being the lynchpin of every high-flying criminal who reached Uruguay from another country, and who had served as a link between the fugitives and the Uruguayan criminal world.

On Friday, 5 November, a police task force, having succeeded in detaining Lentini – on grounds of acting for the 'El Cacho'* gang of juvenile delinquents – finally picked up Heguilein's trail.

This individual was concealed in a house on Cufré Street, where the police took him by surprise in his pyjamas while he was shaving one morning. Despite being surrounded, he fled over the roofs and leapt from the flat roof of an adjacent house into the garden below, where he was finally captured. Nando said he'd left the gang when he became 'horrified at the cowardly way in which they had attempted to bump off Yamandú. I am a man of principles, a political prisoner. I belong to the National Justice Movement (MNJ)† and fight for the return of General Perón,' declared the criminal.

'Yes, yes, of course you do,' replied Police Commissioner Santana Cabris of the Investigations Bureau. 'But primarily you are a vicious Argie bastard who murders my police officers.'

Nando knew about torture, he knew he had to remain silent for as long as he possibly could. Because with the cattle prod, if you begin talking, you find you just can't stop. He was going to try to say nothing at all, not a single word, because he was afraid of having the location of Malito's safehouse forced out of him. Malito counted as his friend, not just any old fellow, he was a true old-style bandit and an idealist, this

---

* *Cacho* means a chub, as in the fish.
† *Movimentismo* was the amalgamation of popular movements that Peronism sought to incorporate. It led to the formation of numerous 'fronts', military or not, but all rigidly disciplined and bureaucratized as branches of 'populism'.

Malito, who could yet become a popular hero after the fashion of Di Giovanni or Scarfó, or even like that Ruggerito or the forger Alberto Lezin and the rest of the wild bunch who'd fought for the nationalist side.* They were going to have to kill him, thought Nando, 'cause he wasn't going to give away Malito's hiding-place.

He tried not to think while they were taking him down to the torture chamber. Nando had decided to keep his mind a blank, white as a new sheet or an unwritten page. They had bound his eyes, and were possibly intending to bring him before the judge within twenty-four hours. He had seen them in uglier moods on other occasions, and this time was certain the press were behind the police and that they would publicize the fact of his being taken prisoner.

The truth was that Heguilein's capture went almost unnoticed in the tight contract between the journalists and police back at Headquarters, when it transpired that they had found the missing face among the Argentine gunmen. It was from

---

* Severino di Giovanni fled Italian fascism and joined an anarchist group in Buenos Aires in 1923. First he simply edited the flagship magazine *Culmine*, but Sacco and Vanzetti's execution in the States turned him to direct action, mainly through bombing North American business venues. Arrested by the police after a fusillade, he was executed on 1 February 1931. The Scarfó brothers were anarchist gangsters, a pair of brothers who raided banks, most famously the National City Bank in 1927. Juan Nicolás Ruggero (known by the diminutive Ruggerito) was the best-known member of a famous mafia family, who ran a gambling den at 400 Pavón Street. He was assassinated in 1933. Lezin, also known as 'the Astrologer', founded a terrorist group intending to seize political power in a putsch. Instead it declined into corruption and infighting and he was killed.

this time on (according to the reporter on *El Mundo*) that the greatest barbecue that had ever been 'roasted' in the police annals of the River Plate division started heating up.

A few hours into the afternoon, in a Buenos Aires province police aeroplane, tourist class, the chief of the Buenos Aires police from Zona Norte, Police Commissioner Cayetano Silva, arrived at Carrasco airport to cooperate with the Uruguayan authorities.

As they taxied down the airport runway, and before descending from the aeroplane, Silva was sifting the information from his colleagues.

'We came across them quite by accident, in a ridiculous incident. They were switching the licence plates on a stolen car.'

'They're on their own. They've no further contacts.'

'Time to put on the pressure.'

'It's not necessary to go around arresting everyone. You need to leave some elements at large and wait until the Argies try and contact them.'

'With Yamandú picked up, they'll be out there, isolated.'

'So,' said Silva, 'if they're out there, isolated, they'll change their plans. What can they do? They'll attempt to leave the city.'

'Impossible, we've blocked all the ways out.'

'It's important to put it out through the newspapers that Yamandú is collaborating with us.'

The investigators had reached the conclusion that Malito and his accomplices were now finding themselves with rather less money in their pockets. The purchase of documents; the expenses of their clandestine transport – in the yacht the *Santa Mónica*, as sources in the police department confirmed – across to Uruguay; the orgies that took place in their refuges; the hiring of cars and the apartments being used as hideouts, had all eaten into their capital. Tales of the orgies were related by Carlos Catania, a rent-boy who presented himself to the police spontaneously, and gave an account of the previous weekend's events. The evil-doers acquired boys and women and quantities of drugs, spending two days in a 'rave', as they called it, filled with 'acts of abject depravity'.

'They're sound,' said the seventeen-year-old, 'they gave me a suit.'

This youth was the first to mention Kid Brignone's visits to the redlight zone around the Plaza Zavala, and his friendship with Giselle.

'I want to speak to that girl alone,' Silva said.

Personnel from the Interior Ministry, exploiting the inexhaustible source of specific references which together make up night life in Montevideo – whisky bars, gaming rooms and the like – thus learnt that the Argie gunmen channelled their attempts to find 'a good place to go to ground' through the mediation of a young escort (the country girl from over the River Negro) who worked in the neighbourhood.

In tandem with the attempts to rent an apartment for a few days, the gunmen were preparing a safe passage into Paraguay, for which they were offering an exorbitant sum. The attempts ended up in the hands of certain persons who owned an apartment in the Liberaij building (at number 1182, Julio Herrera and Obes Streets), who, it transpired, had certain connections with the police world.

A further unconfirmed version relayed that the Argentines had reached the flat thanks to a minor connection with the

Uruguayan underworld and that this contact ('a patsy'), in order to rid himself of the risk posed by the Argentine gang, had acquired the lease on the flat and had immediately 'sold' the information on to the police without the original property owners or their tenants knowing who on earth the birds who had flown to seek refuge in apartment number nine at 1182 on Herrera and Obes Streets really were.

In short, it's a long and complicated story which twists and turns into and out of every nook and cranny of a nocturnal existence, where it's easy – as someone might say out of sheer neighbourliness – for the honest night-club punter to hook up with the smuggler, the assailant and the pickpocket, without realizing what their occupations are. It's left to the police to explain all that. Meanwhile, the one thing that's certain is that the Argentine criminals entered the apartment referred to above only a few minutes after ten o'clock yesterday evening.

Flat number nine is the *garçonnière* shared by the two farmers from the East, who had subcontracted it from the proprietor for a sum of 480 Uruguayan pesos a month. The two farmers are male cousins, both around twenty-five years old. Both, again, habitually frequent the night-club circuit and enjoy the low-life with the rent-boys from the port.

How on earth did the gunmen Brignone, Dorda and the Crow Mereles get as far as this flat, being sought on all sides by the police department? The journalist didn't know but had various hypotheses to propound.

One version recounts that the gunmen had done a purchase deal with their legitimate proprietor (a Uruguayan of Greek extraction), likewise a nocturnal animal, who lived more in Buenos Aires than in Montevideo and whose surname, it was said, could have begun with the letter 'K'.

The gunmen had handed over an initial payment of 80,000 Uruguayan pesos to 'K', without his knowing anything of their real identity, having only met up with them on their nocturnal circuit around the Old City.

Going beyond conjecture, what also seems certain is that the flat on Julio Herrera and Obes Streets was a genuine 'rat-trap' set by the police to attract the fleeing gunmen. No one knows quite how, but through some means or another, the police set things in motion so that the gunmen came to take refuge there.

One source who requested to remain anonymous says that the Argentines confided in another Uruguayan crook who turned out to be a police nark, and that he brought them to the attention of people linked to the Homicide Division.

Another version indicates that it was the police who indirectly placed the flat at the disposal of the Argentines and that they got themselves into their 'lair' without the least suspicion that their Uruguayan protector had sold them to their pursuers. If that's really the case – in which instance, it would be necessary to set aside the other version which says that the Argentines bought the flat with a first deposit of 80,000 Uruguayan pesos – the police no doubt operated cautiously because they knew the lay of the land and the threats posed by the fugitives.

Once these fugitives were surprised on the street, the battle was both inevitable and highly perilous for Montevideans. The police desired a situation in which the criminals would be gathered together and to this end, it was said, they had spread their nets wide from the Headquarters in the desire to hand them an apparently secure apartment on a plate – somewhere central, comfortable, furnished etc. – while the

Argentines awaited the contact who was supposed to transport them, according to what Nando had told them, across to Paraguay.

If this is an accurate account of what transpired, and everything leading up to it, the timing mechanism that went into operation to detain the Argentines was triggered at exactly ten o'clock on the night of the move.

Shortly before the appointed hour, the twenty-one-year-old country girl who occupied the flat during her free hours had dressed in a light-blue-coloured suit and was ready to go out, as was her custom, to the night-club in the city centre where she spent her night waiting for the dawn. She carried with her a black handbag and shoes to match, and there's no doubt she had not the faintest notion of what was about to happen.

It was precisely ten o'clock at night. At that moment the intercom downstairs on the building rang and an unknown voice asked permission to come up and speak to the country girl from north of the River Negro. She pressed the buzzer and let him enter.

The man identified himself as a senior officer from Police Headquarters, according to the night-club girl's story (it transpired her name was Margarita Taibo, alias Giselle).

'Get out of here . . . Leave at once,' the man ordered her.

The girl, followed a short distance behind by the senior police officer, did indeed go straight outside on to the street without even finishing applying her make-up, and the apartment remained empty, like a trap awaiting the arrival of its prey.

It was approximately 10.10 p.m.

The dark girl from north of the River Negro went to the

home of a friend who lived on 25 de maio Avenue, and then, with the friends of this friend, they all went together to the night-club in a car with Brazilian licence plates.

Taking advantage of the fact that they knew the flat, which they then went on to bait as a 'rat-trap', the Intelligence Section of the police service controlled the gunmen's moves from the very start, from the first instant they established the contact which gave them access to taking over the hideout.

According to one version, the police stuffed the place with microphones, because they wanted to discover where the stolen money – some 500,000 dollars – had been stashed. Others said that the surveillance and bugging system antici-pated the arrival of the gunmen and had been used to survey the possibly illegal activities of the night-club owners (basi-cally drugs trafficking, and white slavery). Be this as it may, the attempt to recover the loot is (according to certain sources) the one plausible explanation for the strange flaw in the operation.

As is well known, it's current practice in police proceedings to set 'rat-traps' for crooks. This consists in preparing the ambush inside the house or flat they know will have to be vis-ited for some reason or other and making a surprise entry before a defence can be mounted.

In the present instance, it would appear that an error was made. They prepared the rat-trap the wrong way around, working from the outside in rather than from the inside out. If the police, when they went in to bring out the young occu-pant of apartment number nine, had surrounded the place, they could have denied the criminals access to the immense arsenal at their disposal to resist the siege until the moment reached by the description given in this account.

But the police (from Argentina) were looking for something more. What's most likely is that they wanted to kill them off rather than take them alive, in order to prevent them from incriminating any of the officers who (according to the same source) had clandestinely participated in the operation without receiving the share of the booty promised to them.

What remains certain is that the gunmen's red Studebaker entered the garage downstairs in the building at 10.11 p.m.

Kid Brignone ascended the staircase followed by the Crow Mereles and the Blond Gaucho. The Kid inserted the key into the lock and with a light push the door to the apartment opened.

# 6

The *garçonnière* installed in flat number nine, on Julio Herrera and Obes Streets, is a small complex of near-empty rooms, painted a pale green. The door to the flat (the bell doesn't work so, to get in touch with its occasional inhabitants, it's necessary to do so via the intercom system down at street level) opens on to a narrow corridor where (the youth who wrote the police reports for *El Mundo* pointed out) the doors to other flats are also located. It's on the first floor of the apartment block, which has no lift, being only three storeys high. It is important to bear this detail in mind.

Once inside the flat, the first sight afforded to the viewer is that of a kind of living-cum-dining-room of some four metres by three, on whose left-hand side there runs a kitchen, in which there's finally a window giving on to an inner well intended to provide air and light. The kitchen contains a marble-topped counter with a sink in the middle and cupboards underneath. The visitor who enters this flat will meet with empty walls and scant living-room furniture. The door that ought to separate the living room from the kitchen is also missing.

Next in line, opening on to the living-room, there are three doors leading to the two bedrooms and to the bathroom.

The first of these rooms, overlooking the central well, is the alcove used by the dark-skinned girl from north of the River Negro and in it can still be seen a bed, a shelf and a small wardrobe, a wicker table with a glass top, and a chair. There was nothing else in there at all apart from a small lamp on the shelf and, also on the shelf, a photo of the country girl. The bare walls give the flat that atmosphere of precariousness which such places have.

The next room looks on to a second inner well (for light and air) and is also an alcove which was used by the sub-tenants of the flat, along with the numerous occasional visitors who came, by one way or another, to have the key to the apartment or to have access to borrowing it. There's a double bed in the middle of the room, a toilet to the left and a wardrobe to the right, facing the foot of the bed. To the right, in the middle of the room, another window opens on to the inner well (affording light and air). The basic difference between this bedroom and the other is that the one belonging to the dark-skinned girl from north of the River Negro has polished parquet flooring and its walls are whitewashed, in this room the reverse is the case. The room has no regular incumbents: nobody is bothered to keep it in even a minimum state of cleanliness.

Finally there is the bathroom, containing nothing but the usual fittings, just a General Electric boiler and a blue plastic curtain running around the bath. Above the bath there is a window that opens on to the inner well, affording light and air.

'Across the other side there's nothing at all, only the patio.'

Mereles had clambered on to the edge of the bath and was leaning out, looking downwards from the window. Grey walls, lit windows and beneath them the corrugated iron roof of a shed. The Kid and Dorda headed into the living-room.

'There's a TV here, look . . .'

'Didn't I tell you it was reasonably well furnished . . .'

'Che, what a stink there is in the toilet . . .'

'So,' the Kid continued explaining, 'we went, because you'll remember, Crazy, that before, we wanted to go to Mexico, and I had a friend who went and bought a passport, because he had so many stamps on his, he was called Suárez and was helped by his surname (because every other person is called that) and it was in Mexico they finally bumped him off . . .'

'Listen to me, Rubberlips, who in their right mind would think of going to Mexico . . . The altitude bursts your eardrums, and once in La Paz my snout poured blood simply from opening my bedroom window.'

'But what I'm telling you is that you have to get to New York. There's a highway that runs from the Tierra del Fuego to Alaska, didn't you know that? Look at the map and it's like a thread, running and running, all through the open countryside, the Germans built it, they brought in the diggers, made the natives do the work and you could get from one end to the other by bicycle.'

'I'm going to crash here, chuck over the bolster, would you? Let's eat something.'

They had bought chickens on a spit and whisky and corned beef, enough reserves to last them a week, in case they couldn't move around.

'Hi Che, and is Malito coming over soon?' Mereles was stuffing chicken down him and drinking whisky out of a plastic tooth-mug. 'Should we wait for him? Does the country girl know him or not?'

'I've sent a message to let him know we're here.'

'I saw on the TV that you can rob a cinema if you come in through the rear door, through that little room where the projectionist sits . . . You enter, cut off the exit, fire over the heads of the audience to get them down on the floor, and make off with the loot of all those punters who came in to see a film and then you get out through the window of the projection room. It's perfect, all in darkness, the film keeps on running and covers any noise you make . . .'

'What do you mean, you saw it on television?'

'It was a programme about security lapses in public places . . . Imagine the dosh you could make from a full cinema . . .'

They had to await Malito's arrival with a new car and papers, to leave with him at dawn and head out north, bury themselves in the countryside, hide out in a maizefield in Durazno, or Canelones.

'So as far as you're concerned, it should all be left in the hands of fate . . . If he comes, he comes, and if he doesn't come, then what? It seems a poor deal to me.'

'It's a rough deal, but there isn't another on offer. We have to stick together and wait.'

'If we hold out for a week here for things to die down outside, that'd be better. I like this place.'

'But Malito's due to turn up here by tonight? . . .'

'Listen, if you want to strike out alone, just try it, you're taking a big chance.'

'Don't be an idiot, what do you want . . .'

'Anyway, where do you know this guy from, that flatface who wants to take you off to Mexico?'

'I got to know him in Bolivia, he had a Harley-Davidson 500 with a sidecar and travelled full tilt across the country, shooting at hares with his .45, over arid desert, with his helmet and goggles, the peasants leaned on their spades and exchanged glances, the madman making his bike leap like a spring trying to re-enter a trap, but the bike, you know what they're like, like aeroplanes, those bikes, always up in the air, and the guy was a madman, seriously mad, right, I can tell you that he kept his daughter locked upstairs at his farm because she looked like her mother, the girl did, and the flatface made her dress up in the dead woman's clothes, and walk along in front of him, and I dunno what lots of other things he made her do, and when he went to Mexico he wrote letters to his daughter, she was a stunning looking bitch, you know, that girl, amazing little breasts, and even after they killed the guy, the girl continued receiving love letters from her father, I'd no idea who was writing them, the kid was a real headcase after being mixed up in all that . . .'

Mereles emerged from the kitchen with some packs of cards and a jar of chickpeas. He had stashed the weapons and the loot in the little room next door and they were now ready to spend a quiet night, waiting for Malito to come and seek them out.

'I found some packs of cards, let's play three-handed poker.'

'Let's go . . . every chickpea is worth ten grand, I'll deal . . . Let's see what we get . . .'

At that point they heard a buzzer, perhaps they even heard it before it sounded, an instant before they first heard the metallic buzz and then the voice calling up to them.

They'd been playing cards for a little while, on the wicker table covered with a white kitchen cloth, by the light of a fringed chandelier, in the middle of the room overlooking the street, when they heard the metallic buzzer, sounding like a rat squealing, a devil shrieking, a microphone making a metallic hum as it's first connected and then the voice warning them to give themselves up.

It was the police.

The voice that reached them was distorted, a falsetto, a typical pig's voice, twisted and arrogant, empty of every sentiment apart from those of an executioner. The type of voice used to bellowing, convinced that the other will obey or dissolve on the spot. This is the voice of authority, the one you hear over loudspeakers in the cells, in hospital corridors, in the dungeons where they transport prisoners in the middle of the night, across the empty city down into the police station basements to torture them with lashes and electricity.

Mereles and the Kid exchanged looks.

'The pigs.'

Hearts thumping at a thousand beats, heads feeling as if illuminated by a white light and thoughts grabbing brains like leeches. All for an instant and then it was impossible to feel or think at all. What has to be most feared, the worst thing in life, always happens out of the blue, without anyone being ready for it, which makes it all the worse, because one is both waiting but has no time to get used to the idea and is caught out, paralysed, yet obliged to act and take decisions. The bottom line is that what one most secretly fears always occurs, and all along they had been convinced they had the cops on top of them, or at least breathing down their necks, and that the lair into which they had clambered was too tranquil, too perfect, that they ought to have stayed out on the streets, going round and round in the car until they'd invented a means of escaping the city and the police roadblocks, they'd thought of doing it but had felt too claustrophobic and nobody had said anything, and now it was too late, and they were all corralled in here together.

'We know who you are. You are completely surrounded.'

'Everyone in flat number nine, come out with your hands held high.'

The Kid switched out the lights and the Gaucho leapt across to the little room and began handing out the Thompson, the .9 Falcon, the sawn-off shotgun, spinning them across the floor towards the windows where the Kid and the Crow had holed themselves up.

An icy light came in from the street and illuminated the flat with a ghostly sheen. The white spotlights on the reflectors entered between the slats on the Venetian blinds and filled the air with stripes, luminous rays floating in the dust like a cloud. The three remained, semi-concealed, tattooed by the rays of light, and leaned out of the window, attempting to figure out where things stood.

'It was that little whore . . .'

'And Malito? . . .'

'How many are there? Why aren't they coming up?'

They moved in the twilight and tried to locate the police. Their first sensation was that they were being forced to move blind, encircled by the utmost danger, like someone driving in the countryside at night, sensing he's about to crash, and feeling the air with his hands, as though to divine whether there's an electric current out there, in the midst of all that darkness. The only light indoors was the glow of the television left on without sound. Dorda was in a corner and opened his bag of drugs. He held his machine-gun in one hand while with the other he was chopping up the coke on his watch-face. It was 10.40 p.m.

'We have you surrounded. This is the chief of police speaking. Hand yourselves over now.'

In the darkness the Kid is crouching and cautiously leaning out of the window. In the street shadows can be seen, two patrol cars can be seen, two searchlights illuminating the building's façade can be seen.

'What's up?' asks Dorda.

'We're fucked.'

Dorda puts the machine-gun down on the floor, sits down with his back propped against the wall, opens a small rectangular box of silvery metal, and then in a complicated and rapid manoeuvre shoots himself a dose of cocaine into a vein in his right arm. He does so because he can hear voices in the distance, now, soft voices, women's voices, and he doesn't want to hear them, he wants the whiteness to cure them, the white that rises in his veins wiping the noise of the voices, in the plates of his brain, between his bones, the passages have their own capillaries along which the delicate women's voices are echoing. Dorda hears all of this, all of the time, he tells the

Kid as much, he's trying to speak in a low voice, while the cops deliberate and they deliberate too, at floor level, like rats, stuck in their crevices, in their cracks, squealing, their teeth sharpened, that's where the voices he's hearing come from. Kid. He was raving about rats, about insects infesting the nostrils of dead bodies.

'I saw photos.'

'You saw photos,' sighed the Kid. 'Quiet down, Gaucho, we're going to make them shit themselves, don't listen to what they're saying, keep watch here.'

'Malito, we know you're in apartment number nine. Surrender and come downstairs, we have a magistrate with us.'

Squatting down, the Crow curses under his breath: 'That mad shithead.'

'They think he's up here with us.'

'So much the better,' Dorda's laughing now. 'That way they think there are more of us.' Sitting on the floor, he pokes the gun out of the window. 'Shall a fire off a shot? Just one little shot?'

'Calm down, Gaucho,' the Kid tells him.

Dorda once more chops the drug on his watch-face, using his Spanish penknife with its two blades, lifting the coke on the sharpest edge, raising it with a firm wrist, without trembling, to his nose which flares and inhales, not injecting this time, it's more direct, reaches through the interstices of his skull, the whiteness, the pure air. And this is the only sound in the middle of the night. The Blond Gaucho's avid breathing as he snorts the cocaine.

The police offer a guarantee of safe-conduct to the criminals in the presence of the aforesaid Investigating Magistrate of the Second District Dr José Pedro Púrpura, but the guys don't answer him. The apartment remains in darkness, in silence, the police illuminate the walls, windows, with the patrol car's searchlight as though they were making signals from a lighthouse to a ship, but nobody responds.

Colonel Ventura Rodríguez, the Uruguayan chief of military police, once the house was 'completely encircled' (according to sources) approached the door and used the intercom system – or 'electronic caretaker' – to tell the occupants in flat number nine they were surrounded and should surrender, offering assurances that their lives would be respected. Mereles was now in the kitchen, intercom phone in hand, and the Kid standing at his side. They had opened the door to the freezer and the cold clarity of its spectral glow allowed them to look at one another while they pressed their faces to the receiver to listen.

'Why don't you come up and get us?' shouted the Kid.

'My friend, this is the chief of police speaking, I am the one who is guaranteeing that your lives will be respected.'

'Why don't you come up and play a round of poker with us, Chief?'

'Here is the magistrate who will safeguard your defence, and assures you that you will not be taken to Buenos Aires.'

'But that's what we want, sunshine, to go and fight in Buenos Aires, where that bastard of a Police Commissioner Silva is . . .'

'I can't do any more for you lot. I can only guarantee your lives and a fair trial . . .'

Fresh and worse insults were the only response. At one moment or other they answered that while the police were getting hungry, they were eating roast chicken and slugging whisky, in addition to which they still had three million pesos to divvy out.

'And you, how much do you earn? You'll be killing each other over small change . . .'

Comments made by the criminals demonstrate that they were evidently under the influence of alcohol and drugs. A stream of curses and foul language signalled to the chief of police the impossibility of 'dialogue and negotiation' with those cornered and that the incident was threatening to turn violent. As if in further demonstration of this was the relay of their voices on the building's intercom demanding to know if there were Argentine cops among those surrounding the house, challenging these compatriots to be the first to come and arrest them.

'Bring on the Argentine cops . . .'

'We want the Argie pigs . . .'

It is known that this type of criminal (indicated the police doctor in charge of the first aid post installed at the siege), particularly in the cases of the three who concern us here, is likely to be a drug addict, needing to maintain his habit in order to survive the kinds of conditions in which these three now found themselves. In corroboration of this fact, in a police search carried out later, they found 144 wraps of a drug known as Dexamil Spanzule and various 'raviolis' of cocaine that in their haste to get out the criminals had abandoned there. But persistent consumption can, as we know, induce hallucinations over a sustained period, something it was impossible to verify at this stage of the proceedings.

Further proof that the criminals found themselves in abnormal psychical conditions due to drug abuse was found in the fact that, on encountering themselves in such a difficult situation, today (yesterday) during last night, when the chief of police tried to intimidate them into giving themselves up, they replied: 'No, we're all doing just fine where we are, thanks, eating chicken and drinking whisky, while you lot are standing around outside getting hungry!'

'Why not come upstairs? We're inviting you . . . !'

The Crow signalled to the Kid and they moved back, still crouching down, to one side. They looked at one another, close to, leaning against the wall.

'Do we go out?'

'No. Let them come and get us, if they've got the balls. Malito will soon be here to get us out . . . Something'll happen, he must have run into them a short time ago, when he got near, since the block is bound to be surrounded and he couldn't get through. We have to hold out . . . and make a try for it when they weaken a bit . . . Let's try and make it out on to the flat roof.'

'Where are the cops positioned?' asked the Kid. 'Can you manage to see them?'

'They're all over the place.' Dorda was amusing himself. 'There are about a thousand . . . and they've got lorries, ambulances, patrol cars . . . Let them come up, let them just try . . . It'll be like potting starlings.'

'Lorries, whatever do they want lorries for . . .'

'To take away the corpses . . .' said the Crow and at that instant the firing began.

First there came the dry juddering of a 9-millimetre and then the noise of a machine-gun.

Dorda, squatting by the window, looked out on to the street and smiled.

He was looking out of the window in the unused room,

which opens on to the inner well for light and air, and also looks into the corresponding window of the block opposite, through which the police had opened fire on to the besieged criminals. The round was responded to in kind by the Argentines and was prolonged by intermittent firing, much to the amazement of the entire population of Montevideo who began to follow the events on radio and television.

At a given moment there came a loud shout from one of the criminals.

'One to the door and the others to the upper windows.'

That was the strategy they employed throughout the night.

The apartment's location turned it into a mortal trap. There was no way out. But in its defence, it has to be said that it was the perfect hideout. The sole means of accessing the door was along the corridor and the door itself was protected by a bend in the staircase. Any attempted advance by that route was sheer suicide. The police continually fired down the corridor (there are hundreds of bullet holes in the walls and the plastering has fallen off exposing the brickwork) and the gunmen fired against the wall, mounting a submachine-gun at every one of the breaches opened up by the tracer bullets, in the hope that the projectiles would ricochet off the walls and rebound into the street.

'Once, in Avellaneda, the pigs holed us up in a shed, me and my youngest brother by Letrina Ortíz, and we found a basement leading into the sewers . . . A narrow opening no wider than this,' Mereles demonstrated the size, 'and we got out through there.'

They became energetic, trying to move around without being seen from any of the points controlled by the police. They had put the television on the floor so that it wouldn't get shot up and, from time to time, whenever there was a pause, they watched what was happening in the street. They also followed the account of what was going on on Radio Carve, the heightened register of the voices of their presenters, taking turns to recount the intense moments being lived in the city of Montevideo ever since the Argies occupied the el Liberaij apartment block. People had gathered together in the district, were making absurd statements into microphones and in front of cameras, as if they all understood exactly what was happening and were its actual and immediate witnesses. Thanks to the television screen, the Kid and the Gaucho realized that outside it had begun to drizzle, it was as if they were lost in space, holed up in a kind of capsule, a submarine (Dorda said) that had run out of fuel and was resting on the rocks at the bottom of the sea. The shots were like depth charges that shook them without succeeding in dislodging them.

The police confined themselves to firing at the door, preventing the faintest possibility of escape. They kept up a repeated, terrifying, angled fire at the kitchen skylight which gave on to the inner well. A continuous stream of iron poured through that skylight, barely illuminated in the shadows, whenever one of the criminals attempted to gain access to the kitchen.

'They're never going to get in this way. There are over six clear metres from here to the staircase.'

'So long as we hold out, they can't approach from the front.'

'It was the whore,' said Dorda.

'Don't think so.'

'It's the ill luck we bring with us.'

'You stick by the window.'

'How much dope is there?'

'Malito, surrender, you're surrounded.'

'The buggers think that Stripey is in here with us . . .'

At this moment, through the window, there came a huge explosion, shattering the panes. With it came two teargas bombs.

'Get water . . . from the bathroom.'

They covered their faces with damp handkerchiefs and used wet towels to pick up the two smouldering bombs and toss them back out through the window towards the staircase and down into the hall below. The police and journalists (and the excessively curious) retreated on receiving an unexpected shower of teargas. The police decided to delay before resuming the gas attacks, and to switch tactics. They were going to attempt to gain control of the flat roof on the neighbouring house and, from there, to control the bathroom window.

The police connect up another spotlight which begins sweeping a white light across the room. Mereles fires through the door while Dorda covers the window. The Kid opens the door and leans out on to the corridor.

'D'you see anything?'

He goes to the window which looks out on to the terrace.

'They're going to try and cut us off from the flat roof.' He retreats rapidly, and returns to them. 'From there they can control all the rooftops.'

'They're trying to come in from above.'

'Impossible: if they do that to us, they'll be showering us in shit.'

The three remain calm, seated on the floor with their backs to the wall, covering every angle into the flat; they're simultaneously tranquil and high as kites, full of amphetamines, loaded with every kind of drug. The police are always more fearful than the gangsters, they have to do it all for a salary (according to Dorda), a meagre salary at that, for their retirement years, with the little woman at home whining because her workhorse earns so poorly, has to do night shifts, outside in the rain, who the hell would think of becoming a cop, only a saddo, a guy who has no better idea of what to do with his life, a 'pusillanimous' type (he had acquired the adjective during his time in jail, and he enjoyed it because it sounded like someone without a soul, spirit, anima). They become cops because they want a secure existence and that's how they lose their lives, since, to get them out of here, they were going to approach them calmly, because there was no way they were going to gamble their lives, except that a few of the cops (Police Commissioner Silva, for example) knew that the loot was all stashed inside, and imagined they could get in there ahead of the rest, stick the dosh in their pockets, then say that nothing had been found. 'There was nothing there at all.'

But it was a tricky situation, and the game was up. The Kid decided to tell them they still had half the green stuff left, to be offered as a sweetener to anyone who helped them get away. He had said as much to the chief of police over the intercom, and the message had been broadcast on television, as proof (according to the journalists) that the criminals were willing to gamble the lives of everyone involved in this delicate recovery operation. 'Recovering what or whom?' the Kid had wondered to himself, according to Dorda. 'See how they'll come out with any old rubbish.'

'They're not going to be able to force us out, they'll have to negotiate.'

'To get us out, they'll have to come up the staircase and cross the corridor. It'll be like potting starlings.'

The Kid went into the kitchen and leaned on the buzzer to the intercom, lifted the receiver and began shouting until he heard someone downstairs actually listening to him.

'If that stinking sonofabitch Silva is down there, send him up to negotiate, he can't cry off this time. We have a proposal to make, 'cause if we don't, a lot of people are down to die tonight . . . You've got to get involved, Uruguayan arseholes, at some point in this story . . . We're Peronist activists, exiles, fighting for the General's return. We've a lot of information, Silva, would you like me to start telling them what I know?'

There was a pause, you could hear the cables crackling and the soft hum of the rain, below, but the police down there listening offered no reply.

Silva then approached the intercom and leaned on the buzzer. He wasn't going to speak to those pieces of shit, he was going to spring them from their lair and only then were they going to have to squeal.

'Get us a cab, leave us free to go to Chuy, on the border, and we'll hand over the loot and won't speak to anyone. What d'you think, boss?' said the Kid.

There was a silence, you could hear the Gaucho whistling as if he were summoning a dog, and eventually a Uruguayan police officer approached the intercom and looked steadily at Silva, who gave him a gesture of consent.

'The Uruguayan police do not negotiate with criminals, sir. Surrender and you'll save your lives. If not, we'll be obliged to take even more drastic action.'

'Go fuck yourself.'

'Your rights are protected by the magistrate.'

'What liars you are, you arseholes, as soon as you've got us, you'll stick us into the pan and fry our guts.'

The crowd of journalists registered the conversation on their microphones pressed to the wall surrounding the intercom.

Another crowd of the curious had begun to circulate in the area when they heard the first shots and the TV cameras of the Montecarlo de Montevideo channel had begun a live broadcast, covering events as they unfolded. It even reached the gunmen (as the press had pointed out it would) watching television in their room, watching the events of which they were themselves the protagonists. And in all the neighbouring houses it became commonplace for individuals to shield themselves with cushions to protect themselves from stray bullets, or to hide under their beds, still watching what was happening in their very own neighbourhood. For their part, radios were relaying the siege via live transmissions from flats they had previously rented, and journalists were circulating the immediate environment of the buildings with their microphones permanently on. For hours the entire population of Montevideo was tuned in to the momentous events that were shaking the country.

At 11.50 p.m., three men offered themselves as volunteers, in order to enter and break down the apartment door. After a brief deliberation, the police command accepted their offer and ordered them to take action. Cautiously, Inspector Walter López Pachiarotti, along with Commissioners Washington Santana Cabris de León, in charge of the Department of Investigations, and Domingo Ganduglia, in charge of Division 20a, crouched low and ran across the entrance to the building and advanced along the corridor. The three men went into the central hall in the apartment block, at the far end of which a staircase doubles to the right, and ends up at the doors to flat number nine. Officer Galíndez volunteered himself as an additional fourth man to cover the rearguard action. All four then filed up the staircase, forming a rhomboid in the classic formation of a frontal attack.

Ganduglia went in front with a cocked Uzi submachine-gun, bringing along Santana Cabris on his left and López Pachiarotti on his right, in a protective fan closed by Galíndez at its base, between the two of them. The lights had been turned out and the staircase was a dusky tunnel rising towards the light in the besieged apartment. A sepulchral silence flooded the place, men advanced tense and pitched forward. Suddenly the fourth man at the back tripped on a step and, in falling, grabbed hold of Ganduglia, who fell in turn. That was what saved his life since, through a window to the right of those climbing up the staircase, Dorda had positioned his weapon and now fired off a volley of machine-gunfire, aiming from the floor upwards, hitting Cabris in the thorax and the head and wounding the rest.

'They gave it me, the sonsofabitch . . . my sainted mother,' one could hear the unfortunate man wail while Dorda laughed out loud from the window.

'Pig,' he yelled, 'executioner, I got you. Come on, come on up, shitless Uruguayans . . .'

Facing upwards, with three gigantic wounds in his body and his eyes wide open, in agony, breathing with hoarse groans, in the midst of a horrific haemorrhage, the thirty-two-year-old officer was the father of two children about to be made orphans by his death. Beside him, another wounded man was dragging himself towards the exit, while a third stared at the blood gushing from his chest and could not believe that his ill fortune had brought him to realize his own worst fears. Meanwhile Officer Ganduglia felt no pain at all, only cold, as if his own hand on his belly were made of ice. He had an abdominal wound and didn't even want to look at it.

Beneath the headlamps on the lorries and the outside lamps, in the zone illuminated by the spotlights, lit to prevent the gunmen from slipping away through the windows, the remains of the two dead young men and the third man with the stomach wound were laid out on the pavement. They looked less like two young men who had departed this life (according to the reporter on *El Mundo*) than like something thrown out by a cement mixer, nothing more was left of them than lumps of bone, pieces of intestines, and hanging flesh belonging to those who, it was now impossible to believe, had so recently been endowed with life. For those who die from bullet wounds don't die cleanly as in war films, where the wounded give an elegant sort of pirouette and fall, whole, like wax dolls; no, those who die in a shoot-out are decimated by the firepower and bits of their bodies get strewn across the floor, like animal parts in a slaughterhouse.

The cameras panned across the wounded because for the first time ever in history it was possible to transmit it all live, without censorship, including even the dead men's faces as seen in the battle of law against crime. Should a man prolong dying, his death is dirtier than you could ever imagine: chunks of torn flesh and bone and blood staining the pavement along with the terrifying groans of the dying.

The one who died here (noted Renzi, in his little exercise book) died at once, before his body could register the least surprise or comprehension, only its preceding fear, the fear previous to climbing the staircase towards the flat where the gunmen were holed up.

'They're like rabid dogs. I remember,' said a policeman, 'that when I was a little kid my parents locked our black hound, Wolf, into their bedroom. He was a rabid dog who leapt up the walls in his fury and he had to be killed through the little skylight, slashed with a knife, from above, while he leapt in his madness, that dog.'

'The wounded should be moved now,' said Commissioner Silva, who was observing the scene from the sidelines. 'A wound in living flesh is the worst there is, because the guy endlessly wails and complains, lowering the spirits of the troop.' Then he raised his voice to yell: 'Don't be such a pansy, for fuck's sake.'

But the lad who'd had his leg blown apart carried on howling and calling for his mother. The commissioner was surprised, in contrast, by the measured tones of the young officer with the shot-away stomach who moaned only feebly, with a groan of pain, and raved: 'We entered the corridor and they leapt on us firing. They were nude, drugged, they just materialized like ghosts, about five or six of them. It's going to be tough smoking them out of their lair.'

For his part, the lad with the leg wound was stupefied, as if it were him who was stretched out on the floor of the corridor, wounded; that night he'd agreed to do guard duty in place of a friend who wanted to make a move on the wife of a footballer from Peñarol, away on tour with his team. It was the only night his friend could get near the bitch, and he, like a complete patsy, had agreed to substitute for him and do the guard duty and was now stretched out on the floor shot through with a bullet that had destroyed his leg. Everything was like a bad dream, for over the last two years things had got back on track for him, he had married the woman he had always pursued and had done so despite having to convince her it was worth marrying him even though he was a cop, he had spoken and spoken to her until he convinced her, because she was sickened by the sight of cops, but in the end she resigned herself, seeing that he was much like any other young lad, and, after getting married, they'd bought a little house in Pocitos, with credit from the Police Forces Cooperative Society, but now everything was thrown off track again because the wound was bound to get infested with gangrene and he could see himself with his leg cut off, dragging along on crutches, the turn-up on the right leg of his trousers rolled back to knee-level and held together by a large safety-pin, and then a cold sweat made his teeth chatter and he screwed his eyes up tighter.

Indoors, Mereles is sitting on the floor, his back glued to the wall, with a damp handkerchief tied around his nose and mouth to dissipate the effects of the gases which hover in the stuffy air, although more faintly now, and the Kid is across the room, against the bathroom wall, also seated on the floor, and has set the machine-gun to one side, because weapons get hot with sustained use and can sometimes burn the palms of your hands. That and the sensation of a stomach clenched tight as a fist is the only thing he can feel any more, says the Kid. That and the sense of surprise in remembering the dark girl from the River Negro, the sweet bearer of death. Could it have been her who bore the ill luck that had brought them to this?

'Do you think they could have followed me . . .'

'Don't get worked up about that now. In any case, we didn't have anywhere else to go . . . This country's full of shit, Uruguay has to be smaller than a flagstone, where the hell can you hide in a place this size? I told Malito as much, we should have stayed in Buenos Aires, we had a thousand hideouts there. But here . . . We're cooked.'

'Malito has probably already crossed the pond . . . He has his own streak of luck, a seam of cold blood, on one occasion he went into a police station just when every cop out there was looking for him just because he wanted to lodge a complaint about a neighbour turning up his radio too loud.' Mereles guffawed. 'See how crazy he is, I don't care what you say, he could get through, get in here and pull us out.'

'Or else die along with us.'

'So . . . why not?'

'If he can get in, it has to be because he knows how to get out . . .'

'Oh yeah, in the blink of an eye,' says Dorda, and takes a slug of whisky from the bottle.

They laugh. They don't think any further ahead than the next ten seconds. That's the first thing to learn. It's better not to think about what's going to happen. In order to be able to carry on and not get paralysed with fright, you have to advance step by step, check out how whatever's going on right now pans out, take one thing at a time. Now it's a matter of getting as far as the kitchen and collecting some water. They're not going to let you cross the corridor. Now drag yourself over to one of the windows. They moved around the flat as if it had invisible walls. The police had placed special services marksmen to cover every position and they had had to figure out how to protect themselves, swiftly learning that there were many sites inside the flat at risk from bullets. So they made a sketch, the Crow and Kid Brignone, inside the flat, with a pencil, and traced the lines of fire and saw that it was impossible to cross here and that they had to walk sideways there, as if they were somnambulists, moving as if only in profile, supported by thin air, following invisible corridors, to avoid becoming targets.

'See?' asked Mereles. 'Here's an exit and here's the staircase.'

'Give me cover.'

Dorda stops in the door and begins firing downwards, while the Kid and the Crow slip away towards the passage and search for the fire exit down on to the flat roof.

'Look above you. The roofs are crawling with cops.'

# 7

The lengthy Odyssey which had already lasted for four hours at the time of writing this account began at approximately 22.00 hours yesterday and towards midnight a massive police operation, in which some 300 men were deployed, was mounted. They occupied the flat roofs and the neighbouring houses. Shortly after midnight the gunmen emerged from the flat on to the corridor, where they fired on the street and the nearby terraces, seeking to blaze a way out. An intense blast of shooting was followed by a period of relative calm. The firing from pistols and revolvers diminished in intensity.

A while back they had succeeded in evacuating several of the flats in the building, alerting those unable to leave by telephone that they should remain lying down on the floors of the inside rooms. The police clearly feared that the criminals intended to occupy one or more of the next-door flats and take hostages.

It was possible, in the midst of the gloom, to observe some of the neighbours depart, terrified and in their nightclothes, carrying their belongings. Some of the tenants interviewed by the journalists elaborated the most extravagant theories.

'At first I thought it was a fire,' announced Señor Magariños, wearing a black overcoat on top of his blue pyjamas. 'Then I thought an aeroplane had fallen on top of the building.'

'. . . or the madwoman on the fourth floor,' added Señor Acuña, 'making yet another suicide attempt . . .'

'A black had seized a first-floor flat and was holding two hostages in that apartment.'

'The caretaker's children are dead, poor things, I saw them lying in the corridor.'

During the long hours that this journalist spent in that place information-gathering, all the various versions and permutations got repeated. Some said that Malito had managed to escape from the besieged flat and was going to return with reinforcements, others said that one of the malefactors was wounded. Time passed and the exchanges of fire took place in the middle of the night and under the white glare of the spotlights illuminating the façade and the windows surrounding the flat occupied by the Argentines.

Encircled, hemmed in, with dozens of revolvers and sub-machine-guns positioned at every possible opening and exit, as the hours went by amid the whizz of bullets, the three (or four) gunmen held out, refusing to give in, preferring a defiance born of desperation. They were being fired on from all sides at once. From the flat roofs they were firing at one of the apartment windows; from ground level up at the other one; and from the adjacent flat directly on to the entrance to flat number nine.

It was to be a battle to the death. The flat had been completely cut off and the gangsters were to be laid siege to by starvation, if necessary, although the police didn't cut off the water (or the light) in order not to adversely affect the other tenants. The gun battle was prolonged with interludes when avid members of the public covered themselves from the persistent drizzle in the doorways of houses and were interviewed by the television journalists.

'They're intent on suicide, you can see they won't be taken prisoner.'

'I can understand that. No one who's ever been in jail wants to go back to being banged up.'

'They've got the money in there with them and they'll use it to negotiate.'

The hypotheses and the mutual interrogations multiplied. Meanwhile the siege continued. The block was surrounded, nobody could get in or out of the area, the military barricade isolated the neighbourhood as if it were an island. Everyone had recent images of the Vietnam war in mind. But this time the battle was in a house in the city and the squad being besieged were acting like a group of ex-combatants who had supplied themselves with munitions and weapons of war, prepared themselves to defend their liberty to the end.

The police estimated that between 22.00 hours on the

Friday and 02.00 early on the Saturday the gangsters had fired more than 500 rounds, in their pretence of having a complete arsenal at their fingertips. The PAM submachine-gun, with ultra-rapid firepower, could be heard to resound every few minutes, succeeded or preceded by other firing, with the rattle of a .45 calibre and possibly also of Luger pistols, weapons of war of the highest efficacy.

At one moment it was even possible to hear one of the gunmen yelling that he was going to give a display of all the arms at his disposal. That was when they heard the raking of machine-gun pistols with twelve shots a round, whose detonations clearly demonstrated that they were using large calibre bullets.

The thugs' bursts of machine-guns showed them to be in possession of rapid-fire weapons, because the Zona Norte's chief of police from Buenos Aires, Police Commissioner Silva, said he recognized the sound of Halcón machine-guns, without a doubt stolen from the Argentine Armed Forces. 'It needs to be borne in mind that (on current assumptions) one of the gang members had been a sergeant in the army, and that this was a possible explanation for the possession of these powerful weapons that could hold our police force at bay.'

It was a source of some surprise that these terrible bandits had gained control of such an arsenal, and the police were obliged to question how they could have got it into the country and how they had managed to get themselves from one place to the next across the city, taking so much weaponry and so many thousand projectiles along with them.

Another matter worthy of attention concerning the gangsters' decision is that while it was possible to launch a mass attack of gas grenades through the one window that looked out from flat number nine over the second inner well providing light and air to the block, the gunmen failed to emerge as anticipated. It was then necessary to deduce that they must also possess gas masks, enabling them to resist this otherwise infallible last resort. Or else to imagine a unique resolve on the part of the Argentines who, in the midst of the gas inferno, remained resolute in their resistance to orders to surrender and save their lives.

They no longer have any hope left, resistance is all.

'Why don't you come up and get us?'

'Their courage,' thought the El Mundo journalist, who had taken refuge in flat number eight, adjoining the besieged building, screwing in his flash lamp to obtain night photos of the battle scene, 'is directly proportional to the willingness to die.' The police always act in the conviction that the gunmen behave just like themselves, meaning that gangsters have the same unstable sense of balance when it comes to taking decisions or precautions as does the common man to whom a uniform – representing authority – has been handed, along with a weapon and the power to use it. But there's one crucial difference and it's the same degree of distinction as that between the struggle to win and the struggle not to be overthrown.

Having taken a number of photos, he went over to the corner and leaned against a bench, lit by a street lamp, and took rapid notes in his exercise book.

Quite how the gunmen had succeeded, garrisoned inside the flat, in surviving the huge quantity of teargas canisters thrown at them, was utterly incomprehensible. All the more so to those gathered on the northern corner of the block where the attempted raid was taking place, who could barely tolerate the cloud of gases the breeze was blowing across the street. Certain experts think that the Argentine gunmen possessed (or had made) gas masks, and one even insisted on having seen Dorda, with oxygen tubes and goggles partially covering his face, leaning like a monstrous insect out of the window for an interminable instant and firing off a round before shouting something in a voice which sounded as if it came from the depths of the ocean.

'Why don't you come up and get us, you wretches, what are you waiting for?'

Even the young *El Mundo* journalist succeeded in seeing, almost by chance and as if in a flash, the gunman with his face covered by a complicated gas mask.

The truth is that the lack of oxygen made them nauseous and faint, rather like altitude sickness, or as if the shortage of clean air impeded the blood getting to their brains and sharpened the desperation of their actions. Just now the Blond Gaucho emerged, half naked, through the window, attempting to shoot out the street lamps, along with the bulbs in the spotlights and the searchlights on the patrol cars, leaning halfway into the street, as if nothing more mattered to him than inhaling a little bit of fresh air.

The truth is that gas tends to rise to the ceiling, so that in the lower part of the room, at floor level, it is always possible to stretch out and breathe without serious difficulty. To warm the air and force the teargas upwards the Kid pulled the pillows off the beds on to the glass-topped table and set light to them. The flames gave the place a hellish aspect and the smoke rose and blackened the ceiling and walls. Lying face upwards on the floor, they could breathe easily, the infected air rose over them, like a cloud a metre above their heads. That was the way they got through the night, without major problems, throughout the gas attacks, which were repeated more and more sporadically as the police registered that this particular tactic was not affording them good results.

Everyone seemed to comprehend that the gas, rather than modifying the resistance of the besieged bandits, was hardening their resolve. Their insults could be clearly heard between the din of battle and the incessant rattling of machine-gunfire. The gunmen's resistance was also attributed by certain specialists from the police force to favourable air currents inside the flat which, through the two windows giving on to the two outdoor patios, generated a kind of air corridor which renewed the fresh air available, and sent the polluted air out on to the streets where the effects of the gas were felt by the police themselves, not to mention all the curious passers-by positioned outside.

At one point the police decided to employ hand grenades but were worried about the neighbours still trapped there in the block, since it had not been possible to evacuate several of the apartments in the gunmen's line of fire and the residents were uttering heart-rending cries and calls for help from the adjacent windows throughout the night, for they found themselves in the midst of the din of battle, where they were abandoned and locked up with their children, flattened on the floor without daring to move lest the police commence some sort of salvage operation. They seemed to be currently running the same risks as the criminals.

'In one sense,' Silva declared, his face drawn with fatigue, his white scar whiter than ever in the icy skin of his face, 'the gunmen are holding all the neighbours hostage in the block of flats. And this circumscribes our movements. We have to think carefully what we need to do in order not to put innocent lives at risk. It explains,' he elaborated, 'why this operation is taking longer than the period generally necessary to detain four criminals.'

When the night was well advanced the gunmen made a final attempt to get out of the flat and gain control of the corridor, from where they fired on the street and over the neighbouring roofs, seeking a way out. After that violent gunfight there followed a period of relative calm.

'I never thought we were going to get ourselves stuck down a well and end up hounded like dogs.'

Who did that voice come from? By now a transistor and an intelligence operator, earphones pressed to the heating system, were attempting to find out what was taking place in the besieged flat. But the sound was either dead or muffled and drowned in a confused sequence of signals coming from all over the building: a maddened and tortured multitude of groans and insults with which the imagination of Roque Pérez (the wireless operator) gambled and lost. These were the screams of lost souls writhing in the agonies of hell, stray spirits locked inside the concentric circles of Dante's *Inferno*, for they were already dead, those who, when they spoke, made their voices come through from the other side of life, the condemned, those who have truly abandoned all hope. 'Into what kind of cacophony were their voices transformed?' the wireless operator asked himself, once he could concentrate and began to distinguish out sharp wails, shots and shouts, and again words in some strange language. A dog had been left shut in a bedroom of the next door apartment and barked incessantly. A landscape filled with noise only two centimetres away from his ear drums and across which, like a thread of madness, one could make out the characteristic register, weak and fluting, of a clarinet in a dance orchestra, playing on the radio inside one of the flats, in some remote place that defied location. And alongside all this, the sound of voices, like murmurs of the dead, or words lost in the din of the night.

The person listening in on the conversations was Roque Pérez, the police wireless operator with his headphones pressed to his ears and fingers fiddling with the switches to lower certain vibrations and erase the buzz in the voices, searching to receive their dialogue clean and clear, buried in the tiny soundproofed room in the stairwell, using his levers to control the sound, needing time to establish a sound contact and record the disjointed voices echoing from the apartment under siege. They had planted two microphones, but one had been knocked out by the bullets and transmitted clarinet music as if it had become hooked up to a radio buried in the city. Pérez attempted to identify the voices, figure out who was whom, figure out how many there were, hoping (according to what Silva told him) that one of them would weaken and consider giving himself up, hoping that soon some discord might emerge between the gangsters, and they'd be able to work on one of them, perhaps with an offer of legal privileges, to get him to abandon the gang and surrender. There was a fellow they called Number One who spoke ceaselessly, in a murmur, alone, almost up against the microphone, he had to be over one side, near the heating radiator, the mike concealed close at hand, and Roque Pérez couldn't work out who he was, so he called him One (in fact he was Dorda).

'As for me,' Number One is relating, 'in recent years, when I used to live in Cañuelas, and was out on bail, but I had already left home, and lived on the ranch, I began to collect goldfinches in an aviary and every morning I would release one of them. I'd think that if the birds took note that every day at dawn one of them would be set free, like. I wondered if the little birds had in their eyes a place where they kept their memories, bearing in mind that their sight is as sharp as needles. I thought, I did, of how the little goldfinch sings, then the night arrives, and in the morning a hand is inserted that sets one free, so the other one, let us suppose, his brother, let's say a brother goldfinch, gets animated, takes note, says, "I'll decide to sing all day long, then the night falls so I'll sleep a while, and when the sun is up, a hand will appear and set me free in the open air, leave me free just to fly away."' There was a prolonged pause or the sound of some interference. 'Just like us humans locked away, yet we too hang on to the hope that, come sunrise, something new and good will dawn.'

'And it's not always like that.'

'No, it's not always like that . . . True enough. Do you want some? I've got it. A piece of luck, wasn't it, that we've got some, that I bought some weed, in the port, on our way out, from the seadog who brought us here, a kilo and a half, dope of the first order, higher than top quality, say I, it's always worth having too much rather than too little.'

They chatted on about anything at all, about how the goldfinches had flown free. None of that mattered for now, he (Roque Pérez) didn't want to record the sense, only the sound, the differences between their voices, their levels, and their breathing, in order to learn to identify each one in turn.

'Somewhere out there, and we can't say when but perhaps when the sun comes up, Malito will turn up, Gaucho, and he'll get us out.'

'So Number Two isn't the Crow,' noted Roque Pérez, 'the Crow has to be Number Three or Number One. And the one speaking is Two' (that makes Kid Brignone Number Two).

'A marble headstone on the tomb of the deceased, my father, I had to sell the goldfinches to pay for it, he was in the soil, without anything, just a little barbed wire fence around the patch, the old woman buried him there, we had a plot of ground there on the slope down to the flowerbeds outside the station, where the cemetery ended up, out at Cañuelas, the saddest place in the world, as soon as the graves began to get dismantled by people eager to move in, set up their home-steads and live there, among the dead.'

'They're delirious,' thought Roque Pérez. 'Too many drugs, too many hallucinogenics, old-style hallucinogens at that. They take cocaine, they shoot up everything, they can put up with anything, it's the only way they can cope with the world,' said Roque Pérez, 'they act the macho because they're high on whisky and speed.' Pérez had studied medicine, but entered the police force because he enjoyed wireless operat-ing, he was a great radio fan and trained himself as a technician working in sound rooms and recording studios, and he'd had to get used to living boxed into a cabin, deciphering radiophonic conversations, useless dialogues in order to locate illegal card sharps, police informers, politi-cians who don't want to compromise, minor matters, but now, ever since Friday night, he had got his great opportu-nity: the live secret transmission of what was going on inside apartment number nine, laid siege to by the Montevidean police. Voices, groans, moans, intermittent cries for help, isolated wails. For example, at the moment, there's Number Two:

'Tuesday will be the funeral, they always bury you three days after you die, 'cause if you come back again, you come back to life as a mummy, d'you remember the mummy, who came out of tomb all wrapped in bandages . . .'

'For example, you can hide yourself underneath the bathtub, they'll come and search, and they'll never find you . . .'

'Look, see, this machine isn't functioning properly,' the speaker stamps on the floor and the image settles down again, 'but take a look, it's crawling with journos . . . If you give yourself up, they can't get away with killing you.'

'They'll kill you either way, arsehole,' says Number Two. 'They shoot you here and drag you out dead, however many journos there are out there . . . anyway all journos are narks . . .'

And the cub reporter Renzi in flat number eight noted: 'The agonized waiting period extended. Exhaustion finally took hold of the policemen. The exchange of fire is no longer as intense. There are lapses of fifteen or twenty minutes during which not a single shot can be heard. Then a few stray shots from the marksmen positioned on the ground floor and the flat roof of the shed prompted the gunmen to respond with another volley.'

Then suddenly, unexpectedly, there was an audible pause over the intercom to the block, followed by the wound of one of the criminal's voices, saying: 'Greetings to Commissioner Silva. Silva! Are you there, sweetheart, flatface, executioner, bastard . . . Porky, Silva, come up here . . . why don't you come and play a round for the General's wife?* Who wins get out of here alive, who loses shits himself. There's five hundred grand in the bank, and I'll play you for it on a single throw of the dice. Hear them?' And it was true, you could hear the little marble bones rattling in their leather thimble.

'Enough fucking about, Che, it's me here talking to you. It's me, Silva,' says Silva, tranquil, in his creole accent, in a voice clouded and wasted with alcohol and the quantity of cigarettes smoked during interrogations, attempting to soften up a swindler, a whore, or some poor lottery fixer. It was always the same, year in year out, paying them back with blows to the stomach as they're tied to their chairs, shouting at them in that rasping voice, like someone attempting to stick a pin into the ear of a zombie who refuses to parrot what one wants him to say. 'Why don't you lot come on down? Who's talking to me? Is that you, Malito? Come on down and we'll sort it all out, man to man, we'll negotiate here before the magistrate, I guarantee you, and I won't press charges for armed resistance as part of an illegal gang.'

'Well, why not just come up yourself? Hurry on up. Your daughter is getting it up the arse and you out there like an idiot, they've got her there in the bar toilet, the guy's a thin

---

* This is a deliberate pun: *la generala* is a game of five dice, where the winner is he who achieves the highest score of the same number. But *la generala* is also Evita Perón, nationalist heroine of the right-wing *Peronistas*.

fellow with a shaft thick as your arm, and she's giving squeals of pleasure and shitting herself the more she gets off on it.'

That's how they spoke, filthier, more crude and brutal in their speech than even the cops, for all their experience in inventing insults intended to humiliate prisoners to the point where they become useless floppy puppets. Tough guys, from out of the toughest jails, broken on the electric grill, surrendering at last, after being forced to listen to Silva insulting and applying the torture machine to them for hours on end, to get them to spill the beans. The dead ends of the phrases used by men and women in the bedroom, in business and in the toilets, because the police and the crooks (so Renzi thought) are alone in knowing how to make words come alive, so much so and so sharp they can split your soul apart like an egg breaking on the sharp edge of a frying pan.

'It's not about money,' Number Two is saying and Pérez records the conversation, feeling as awkward as someone involuntarily spying or listening in on an unexpected confession, which is now being broadcast to everybody, Pérez included, who all listen awkwardly, to Number Two telling Silva: 'I'll hand over the money if you get your ugly mug up here, I'd let you come up and go back down without touching a hair of your head, but to get us out of here you're going to have to sweat a bit, after all who d'you think you're dealing with? You, Silva, what d'you want if you come up? Come on up, Che, you're used to screwing thieves when you've got them tied up, but when there's an armed opponent, a tough guy with balls, you crumple, Silva.'

The conversation continued on much the same lines, as if

it were an extension of the combat. Witnesses to the conversation were frozen to the spot, hypnotized by what they were hearing, while Silva attempted to prolong the dialogue, to give Pérez time to record the voices and locate each one of the speakers, this was the reason why Silva sought to get his interlocutor (the Kid?) to continue doing battle over the intercom. And that voice so clearly belonging to a rent-boy, a criminal, a lunatic, rose again through the walls and reached all those gathered in the drizzle and in front of the encircled building.

'At approximately 03.30 hours today (for which read yesterday) the conversation was interrupted, despite the authorities' attempts to keep the intercom open and continue negotiations with the gangsters, they began hearing loud shouts from the criminals who were about to launch a bravura gesture, assuring them they were on the point of emerging prepared to kill any number of pigs and to some extent they began fulfilling their threats as it seemed as if one of their number – in the shelter of the shadows reigning in the corridor of the apartment block – got as far as the middle of the staircase and fired off a violent volley towards the street with a machine-gun.

'This made them think the criminals were about to come out, as the gunfire increased still further, cutting off the entrance to the apartments with a shower of lead.

'This was followed by a moment of despair during which those in the hall ran for the street. They left behind them a man who had fallen to the ground, bleeding heavily from four bullet wounds. It was Inspector Washington Santana Cabris de León, the Uruguayan chief of police. For the space of a few minutes he lay stretched out where he fell, given that the whole area was under a hail of the criminals' bullets.'

'You've sung your song, birdie . . . As for you pieces of shit, why don't you come up and take a look?'

Gaucho Dorda, half-naked, went out into the corridor, placed his gun on the man's neck and, in the midst of an infernal shooting, killed him with a bullet in the mouth. The police chief and the lunatic, degenerate, psychotic, Dorda the recidivist criminal (according to police sources) stared at each other for an eternity and then the Blond Gaucho, just before polishing him off, winked an eye and smiled at him.

'Die, arsehole,' said Dorda, and leapt smartly backwards.

The inspector's face was erased by the firepower as if it had exploded from inside his mouth and ripped the flesh outwards, leaving only a bloody hole behind (or so said an eye-witness).

After the initial shock, the first aid services rushed to remove and take him to hospital in a patrol car, where he was pronounced dead on arrival.

'The critical tactic employed by Malito's gang, its tragic glamour,' (as Renzi was to later describe it in the police pages of his diary in El Mundo), 'fed on the conviction that every victory achieved under such impossible conditions increased their capacity to resist, and likewise increased their speed and strength. This was why what followed had the aspect of a tragic ritual that no one who was there that night could ever forget.'

First some white smoke emanated through the tiny bathroom window that opened, like an eye, above the party wall between the flats. A thin column of white smoke, against the further whiteness of the mist.

'Burning money is ugly, it's a sin. *E peccato*,'* added Dorda, in ecclesiastical Italian, and with a 1,000-peso note in his hand, there in the bathroom where he'd been taking speed, holding a Ronson lighter he'd pilfered from a crazy girl; he took it and burnt it, then looked at himself in the mirror and laughed. The Kid stood in the doorway, watching him and saying nothing.

'Just think: to earn a bill this size, a security guard, for example' – security guards are always contracted in, and they know it, they always catch up with the crooks once they've got into the place through the skylight, that's when the fellow appears, an inane grin on his face – 'would have to work for a fortnight . . . and a bank-clerk, depending on his seniority, would have to work at least a month to get a bill of this size, as he whiles away his life counting other people's money.'

In contrast, they had wads and wads of notes, all of their own. The pills were now dissolved, crushed and disappearing in a glass of Calcigenol, looking like a glass of milk, but tasting very different. The loot was in the bathroom, ready to burn in the basin. The Kid is laughing aloud. Dorda also laughs, if a little fearfully, at what he's cooking up.

It was then, at some point or other, at some given moment, it became known that the criminals were setting fire to the five million pesos remaining to them from the raid

---

* In Italian in the original. Much of what is said takes place in *lunfardo*, harbour slang of the Neapolitan immigrants. *E peccato*, resonant of the Latin Mass, means both a sin and a shame in the colloquial sense of 'what a pity'.

on the San Fernando Town Hall from which, as is well known, they seized seven million.

They began tossing burning 1,000-peso bills out of the window. From the kitchen skylight they succeeded in floating the burning money down towards the corner. The bills looked like butterflies of light, flaming notes.

A buzz of indignation rippled through the crowd.

'They're burning it.'

'They're burning the money.'

If the money were the sole justification for the murders they committed, and if what they did, they did for the money they were now burning, that had to mean they had no morals nor motives, that they acted and killed gratuitously, out of a taste for evil, out of pure evil, that they were born assassins, insensate criminals, degenerates. Filled with indignation, the citizens gathered to observe the scene, offering shouts of horror and loathing, looking like something from a witches' sabbath straight out of the Middle Ages (according to the papers), they couldn't bear the prospect of 500,000 dollars being burned before their very eyes, in a move that left the city and the country horror-struck, and which lasted precisely fifteen interminable minutes, which is exactly how long it takes to burn such an astronomical quantity of money, those notes that, for reasons beyond the authorities' control, were destroyed on a metal sheet called, in Uruguay, a 'hub' and which is used as the brazier for the grill in barbecueing the Sunday roast. It was in just such a 'hub' that the money went up in smoke, and the police stood by in stupefaction, for what could they do with criminals capable of such outrageous behaviour? Scandalized, people's minds indignantly and immediately turned to the poor, those lacking in basic necessities, the rural population of Uruguay living on the margins, and to the little orphans whose futures could have been secured by that very amount.

'If they had only saved the life of a single one of the orphaned children, they would have given some sort of point to their existence, the cretins . . .' announced a lady, 'but they are evil to the core, bad from the innards out, mere animals,' the journalists were told by the eye-witnesses, and the television cameras rolled, then transmitted all-day-round repeats of the rite which the TV presenter Jorge Foister labelled an act of cannibalism.

'Burning innocent money is an act of cannibalism.'

If they had given away the money, if they had thrown it out of the window at the people gathered on the street, if they agreed with the police to hand it over to a charitable foundation, everything would have gone differently for them.

'For example, had they donated those hundreds of thousands to improving prison conditions where they themselves are going to be held . . .'

As it was, everyone understood perfectly well that this was a declaration of all-out war, a direct attack, a textbook case, waged on society as a whole.

'They should be hanged.'

'They should be left to die slowly, burnt to a crisp.'

The idea got out that money is innocent, even when acquired as a consequence of death and crime. It couldn't be considered culpable, but rather it should be viewed as neutral, as a symbol that comes in useful depending on how one wants to use it.

The notion also began to circulate that the burnt money

served as an example of murderous madness. Only crazed killers and immoral beasts could be sufficiently cynical to burn 500,000 dollars. Such an act (the dailies said) was worse than all the crimes that they had committed, because it was an act of nihilism and an example of pure terrorism.

In statements made to the magazine *Marcha*, the Uruguayan philosopher Washington Andrada signalled that however terrible one might consider it, such an action, a kind of innocent *potlatch* let loose on a society with no memory of such a ritual, an act absolute and free in itself, a gesture of sheer waste and sheer outpouring, would in other societies have been taken as a sacrifice made to the gods because only the most valiant is worthy of sacrifice and there is nothing more valiant between ourselves than money, so said Professor Andrada, and he was at once summoned by the magistrate.

The manner in which they burnt the money is proof absolute of their evil genius, because they burnt the money by rendering clearly visible the bills of 1,000 pesos which gradually took light, one after the next, the 1,000-peso bills burned like butterflies whose wings are touched by the flames of a candle and beat for another second as they flare, flying on through the air though consumed by fire for an interminable instant before burning out and turning to ash.

And after all these interminable minutes in which they say the notes burnt like flaming birds before transforming into a heap of charcoal, a funeral pyre to our social values (as declared an eye-witness on television), a wonderfully beautiful column of azure ash raining from the window in a shower resembling the calcified remains of the dead that get scattered across the ocean, or over the mountains and woods, only not over the filthy city streets, for ash must never drift on to the stone floor of our concrete jungles.

In the wake of this act which hypnotized then paralysed everyone, the police came round first, reacting by launching a brutal offensive as if the time in which the Nihilists (as the newspapers now called them) completed their blind ritual had dazzled and delayed them, yet also left them prepared and further inclined to achieve the final hecatomb.

# 8

Weary with issuing useless orders, Commissioner Silva had
stayed quiet for a while. He was at the control post, dressed in
his white mackintosh, leaning on one elbow, alone and smoking a cigarette. He observed the darkened windows of the flat
and saw the hesitant silhouettes of the malefactors, up there,
still holding out. It was essential to kill them and prevent
them from talking. About what? Had there been negotiations?
'Is it true, Police Commissioner,' the reporter on *El Mundo*
noted down the questions in his exercise book, 'that some
policemen, as has been said, arranged the malefactors' flight
out of San Fernando in return for a cut of the booty?'

Silva was the man responsible for having let the Argentines escape, and now every Uruguayan police officer who fell would be counted against him. The lad who wrote the police reports for *El Mundo* observed him from the middle of the street. That face, with its scar, its disdain, loneliness and wickedness, all lodged in the dead glint of his eyes. He caught a fleeting expression of anxiety in Silva, a look he swiftly wiped from his face. The commissioner hadn't allowed himself more than a moment to cover his eyes with the tips of his fingers before shooting another sideways glance at the front of the house illuminated by the beam of the spotlights. A cold glance of a hard guy, a look too fleeting to be faked (according to Renzi) and yet too deliberate to be entirely natural. How many years and how many inner struggles had it taken to perfect that kind of gesture of feigned unease?

From out on the street, the reporter studied Silva's fragile appearance, which resembled a Japanese mask. His delicate hands, 'the hands of a woman', the pistol in his left hand cocked at the ground, like a hook or a prosthesis necessary to complete an imperfect human form. Armed with a weapon he could bluff anyone, he could confront the journalists who were even now beginning to surround him and to join him in gazing up at the half-open window to the hideout. The lad from *El Mundo* began taking notes on Silva's latest declarations.

'They are mentally ill.'

'Killing mentally ill people is not kindly looked upon by journalism in general,' noted the reporter with irony. 'They are supposed to be taken to the asylum, not executed . . .'

Silva stared at Renzi with his weary look; yet again the disrespectful and tedious adolescent, with his glasses and his unruly hair, his puppy face, so alien to the real world and the dangers of the situation, who'd landed like a parachutist, behaving like a professional solicitor, or as if he were a convict's kid brother complaining at the way criminals get treated in police stations.

'And killing healthy people, that's kindly looked upon?' answered Silva in the listless voice of someone being called upon to explain the blindingly obvious.

'Have you offered them a negotiated way out?'

'How can you negotiate anything with criminals like these? Or haven't you been here during the past night?'

'The cops have started to get jumpy,' someone announced.

'And with reason. We're not going in and we don't need martyrs . . .' said Silva. 'Even if we have to hold out for a week, we are going to maintain calm. Those gentlemen up there are psychopaths, homosexuals . . .' he glowered at Renzi, 'clinical cases, human waste.'

'They're made of ice, they have no pity, they're dead' (Silva was thinking). 'They're like living cadavers hellbent on just one thing, discovering quite how many of us they can take with them. They're a miniature army. Adrenalin helps them to overcome terror. They are covered with pinpricks from their needles, they've become no more than killing machines. They want to suss out the limits of what they can get away with, they'll never surrender, they'd sooner make us eat dirt. They've got no normal sense of danger, they carry death in their bloodstream, they've killed innocent people on the streets since the age of fifteen, they're the sons of alcoholics and syphilitics, headcases, simmering with resentment, desperate delinquents more dangerous than a whole command unit of professional soldiers, they're a pack of wolves gone to ground in someone's house.'

'This is a war,' declared Silva. 'You have to bear in mind the tenets of war. Never allow combat to cease when one of your men has fallen. If a man falls, you have to continue. Otherwise what else is left for you to do? Survival is the sole glory of war,' went on Silva. 'And I want you to understand what I am saying. We have to wait.'

Silva intuitively understood the gangsters' way of thinking. Obviously, he was closer to them than to these cub reporters, queers and mummy's darlings the lot of them, would-be heroes, but in reality pedants, ill-born and ill-bred.

'And you, what do you do?' Commissioner Silva turned back, unexpectedly, towards Renzi.

'I'm a correspondent on the Buenos Aires *El Mundo.*'

'I can see that much but, aside from that, what do you do? Are you married, d'you have kids?'

Emilio Renzi moved to one side, awkwardly leaning his weight on to his left foot, and smiled, surprised.

'Nope, no kids. I live alone on the corner of Medrano and Rivadavia Streets, in the Almagro Hostel.' He fished for his documents in his jacket pocket, as if the cop was coming to arrest him. That was where he had gone too far, certain now that the fellow had already marked him down ever since the press conference back in Buenos Aires.

'I'm a student and I earn my living as a journalist, just like you earn yours as a police officer, and if I'm asking you questions, that's because I want to give an accurate account of what's going on.'

Silva studied him in amusement, as though the lad were some sort of circus clown, or a ridiculous mental defective.

'An account? An accurate one? I don't reckon you have the balls for all that,' Silva laughed as he went over to the tent where the Uruguayan officers were meeting to plan the forth-coming attack.

It was true that the only way to break the criminals' grip was to begin thinking like them, and Silva was convinced the gang, cornered like rats in a sewer with no way out, were determined to act the hero and doping themselves in order not to surrender and come downstairs.

For example Mereles, alias the Crow, whose record he was well familiar with, as you could imagine, had always killed just because, because he was shit-scared, he wasn't a man, he was a bloodthirsty puppet, he beat women, there were a number of outstanding reports from women who'd gone with him. 'Courage is like insomnia,' Silva thought, 'you never know which of your worries will seize hold of your mind and persuade you to act the hero.'

Surely they must have spent their lives watching war films and were now acting as if they thought they were a suicide commando unit fighting behind opposing battle lines, in for-eign territory, surprised in their flat by the Russians the other side of the Wall in East Berlin, surrounded and resisting until someone or something came to their rescue, he imagined, and who better than Mereles. There existed a number of sto-ries of military squads who penetrated enemy territory and managed to get through. Survival tactics for a Pacific island and for the apartment on a block where gas floated all the way up to the ceiling and keeping your flanks covered had to be a lot better than a beach-head in Vietnam.

'In *The Sands of Iwo Jima*,'* the Crow sounded all at once

---

* A John Wayne film from 1949, where the action is set on a Japanese

delirious, 'the guys throw themselves down a well and survive a tank onslaught.'

Dorda wanted to sleep a while and at moments he thought he was dreaming of trailing across the countryside, as a kid, hunting hares.

'And what the fuck is *The Sands of Iwo Jima*?'

The gang, survival, squalor, solitude, isolation, imminent danger, fellows who tumble into a well during an ambush.

Sometimes they conversed in a distant murmur, each one to themselves, and at others they bawled orders, exhausted no doubt, with ever more frequent assaults, then rising again to adrenalin-induced euphoric peaks in their bloodstream as night fell and the sun began to whiten, just faintly, the waters of the river on the other side of the town.

'When you're at the front, shafted, and you no longer give a shit, what you have to do is to carry on. It's the only way forward.' That was Number Two speaking.

'Blocked in, backs against the wall, putting your head outside only occasionally, you feel that thinking serves no useful purpose, what'll you think anyway, the more things go round and round in your head, the less you find a way out, if I do this, or if I try that, maybe go out into the corridor, and all the time running into a brick wall that cuts you off, you're down and out, and you have to get up and get a grip, then set to, again – no?' says Number Three. 'Let's hope that Malito has got away and is watching what we're up to . . .'

---

island. It was seized from the Japanese by the US forces in 1945 after battles that took over 100,000 Japanese lives. It was restored to Japan only in 1968.

On the television set they can see the dark-skinned girl saying that she had nothing to do with any of it.

'I'd no idea that these were the Argentines the police were looking for, I got to know one of them on the Plaza Zavala quite by chance, and then two of them raped me . . . But I never handed him in . . . There's nothing worse,' went on the girl, her serious face looking straight to camera, 'than being a stool-pigeon.'

Gradually, the dawn of a new day began to win out over the darkness. The criminals slowly reduced their firing from their provisional lair. The police in charge of the operation gathered round to peruse new battle plans. The crowd of the curious, kept at bay by the rain and cold, began to increase in size once more. The criminals seemed to be resting, keeping one of their number on guard duty, anticipating a possible final attack. From time to time they fired a few rounds to show they were still alert.

From all this, the police deduced that the gunmen, well-stocked with ammunition and ready for anything, were capable of maintaining their position to the last, which was why their attack strategy began to modify as the hours passed. They began to toy with a number of options, talking of launching a grenade of relatively low potency; of injecting the apartment where they were holed up with chemical products used to tamp down fires and which stick to the skin like liquid rubber or napalm, something they definitely would have used had the gang members emerged from their den; of making a breach in the roof in order to be able to fire directly down from the apartment overhead on the second floor; or to open up a hole in the wall adjoining apartment number eight on the first floor, with the same intention of firing on them from in there. The seconds of uncertainty dragged on into several minutes.

Whenever the Gaucho was drugged, he swore to give up drugs, for that was when he believed himself capable of doing so because he was no longer propelled by the wild desire for fresh supplies and thought that a life lived in pursuit of his dealer wasn't a life worth bothering with. The problem was that once he lacked drugs, he couldn't give up, when he didn't have them, he couldn't even think of giving up, he thought only of one thing, of pursuing and obtaining drugs. And the worst of it was, he suddenly realized, horror-stricken, as if yet again the damned voices which had remained quiet for a while had now woken up in order to alarm him, what he finally realized was that if they remained banged up there, sooner or later they were going to find they'd run out of drugs altogether.

'The gear,' he observed, 'is going to run out sooner or later, because however many grams there are, even if we ration ourselves like in a shipwreck . . . you know, once I saw a guy like that on television, who said he'd taken water daily from a teaspoon, so that the water wouldn't run out, on their desert island.'

'On a teaspoon? On a desert island? Water? They sipped it?'

'Like tea.' The Gaucho made a gesture of lifting a teaspoon, little finger crooked, sipping like a bird.

The Crow laughed: he hadn't left the window the entire night through. He had spread his supply of Florinol out on a newspaper and continued taking one every so often, while the apartment floated in a pearly cloud around him.

'Time to get out,' it sounds to the Gaucho like a voice

emanating from an oracle. Gaucho Dorda listens to a chorus of voices issuing orders, voices so subdued you can scarcely hear them, least of all once the firing starts up.

'You know, Kid, they don't speak when there's a racket going on, I can't hear them, they get erased, that's right, then all of a sudden those bitches start nagging again.'

'We've got some *maconha*.'

'*Maconha*?'

'I used to live in Brazil, mate, didn't I tell you? There they call grass *maconha* . . . this lot came from Paraguay . . . the dark-skinned girl gave it me . . . she kept it safe in a tin box in the kitchen, she did . . .'

The Kid got himself across the flat, along its invisible passages, crossing doorways, and finally reached the kitchen where he stumbled into the sideboard, rummaged around with his hand, and pulled out the tin, with its sweet scent of hash. '*La Cucaracha, La Cucaracha*,'* the Kid returned singing, '*ya no puede caminar, porque le falta, porque no tiene* . . . ,' the radio operator was convinced he could hear him singing, Roque Pérez, from some corner of the building, someone, at least, was definitely singing this Mexican *corrido* from the Civil War period.

'This toilet is totally flooded. You have to pee in this bucket and we'll chuck it out of the window on to the heads of the pigs . . .'

'Where did you get the grass?'

---

* Perhaps the most popular *corrido* (ballad) of the Mexican Revolution (1910–20) and a staple of dancehalls thereafter. The *cucaracha* (cockroach) of the title was apparently President Obregón, famously addicted to his marijuana.

'It was that little whore's, she brought it in from Paraguay . . .'

They lit some joints and settled down to watch television. The bullets scarcely reached this side of the flat, close to the way out, and whenever the inmates stayed quiet for a while, the cops became nervous and started firing into the air.

'Look, they've got an armoured personnel carrier, and there's around a thousand of them.'

In the dawn drizzle you could see the squad and the lorries and the journalists on the pavement; the television showed it through a grey corrugated ridge of lines.

'But they're not going to get us out of here. They're going to have to negotiate.'

They were waiting for Malito. Perhaps it was true he had taken a hostage, the son of some aristocrat, and all of a sudden he'd appear on the television screen demanding their release. He was going to come and get them out, he was going to arrive with reinforcements, Malito was. The heavy squad, it'd be, Brazilians from Rio Grande do Sul. He was their mafia boss, was Malito, crazy but highly intelligent, always keeping his distance, not giving a fuck, but straight down the line with his own people, someone who'd never leave them in the lurch, if they could have soaked him by simply lifting up the receiver on the intercom and saying: 'I've got a meeting with Malito on 18 de julio Street.' The dark-skinned girl could have told him about it. As for Malito? Did he know she had a room in a boarding-house near the Mercado? Very much under surveillance just now. They had seen her appear numerous times on television talking nonsense and accusing all and sundry of raping her. Lies to throw them off the scent and get herself off the hook.

'Baby,' said the Kid, and he was talking to the girl's image onscreen. 'Quiet down, skinny, don't keep gassing.' She looked straight at him, from out of the screen, and the Kid disappeared to the back of the flat and put the Winco on with the record by Head and Body:

> *And if I can find a book of matches*
> *I'm goin' to burn this hotel down . . .*

The Kid was singing along with the chorus to 'Parallel Lives'.

The sounds of the night mingled with the dead music of the city itself. Was that Mereles' voice? Number Three's voice? Or could it be Number Two's?

'Once I was trapped down a well for four days. I fell in as a kid and was stuck in there with all these insects crawling over my face and I couldn't shout because I was scared they'd get into my throat and in the end I was rescued by my dog who dug like crazy around the edge of the well.'

Who was that talking? Roque Pérez's universe was growing narrower all the time; there was no space left in the diminutive control room where he was in charge of manoeuvres: he was constrained to follow the almost inaudible sounds emanating from the skeleton of the building. They generated a level of interference and were therefore connected with the spirit of an entire city. The voices travelled along interior canals, because inside the spider's web of the intercom the police had planted two microphones (or was there just one? one solitary microphone up there in the air?). They had installed them to pursue the paths taken by the drugs circulating through the night-clubs, and now they were using them to pursue the traces of these malefactors, although it was possible that they had placed him, Pérez, there in ten-hour shifts, to catch the secret the Argies were still concealing and the police chiefs wanted to elicit before killing them off. But there were additional voices coming in from the other side he couldn't decipher. Perhaps from the past, the radio operator was wondering. Maybe the words of the dead navigate their way through the subterranean sewage system and make it possible to follow the terrified prayer of two old women who'd locked themselves in the bathroom of some apartment or other.

'Holy Mary, Mother of God, pray for us sinners . . .'

Where did this recital of the rosary come from, perhaps from the wireless operator's own memory, perhaps it was the voice of one of the gangsters, or the lamentation of a neighbour. He continued recording all these sounds, and next to him someone was trying to pick their way through the morass of voices. He couldn't leave, he was surrounded, he felt like a spy during the war, sending out messages from behind Japanese lines. A Uruguayan policeman, Corporal Roque Pérez, wireless operator by profession, dropped into the Battle of the River Plate. And if the gunmen took control of the building and discovered him, up there in his little attic, they'd execute him with a bullet to the back of the head at five metres.

Every five minutes (approximately) the police employed microphones to intimidate them with a deafening blast, part of a psychological operation designed to make the pressure unbearable, while the technical corps of the Uruguayan State central intelligence service, using transmitters supplied by the SODRE,* listened in (despite the interference on the line)

---

* Servicio Oficial de Difusión, Radiotelevision y Espectáculos, answerable to Uruguay's Culture and Education Ministries.

on the conversations of the besieged, courtesy of the three microphones hidden in the apartment only hours before it was surrounded.

'There's no death penalty in this country.'

'The death penalty . . . I can't understand the idiot who'd allow himself to be caught so that he could be strapped to a chair and cooked . . .'

'You can be caught by them without meaning to be.'

'Never.'

'They seized Valerga when he was asleep and when they grabbed Beretta, they tackled him so he couldn't escape.'

'There are only four methods of execution: hanging, firing squad, gas chamber and electric chair. You can wait ages to die. Sometimes as much as a minute, a minute and a half . . . Hold your breath and imagine it. The chair itself is pretty sinister: the smoke rising from your burnt skin has an unforgettable odour, it smells of roasting meat. They attach electrodes to the head and legs of the condemned man. You don't see flames, instead you see a change in the skin's colouring as it turns maroon, then black.'

'And in Argentina, what's the system there? D'you know what it is? A bullet in the balls!'

Dawn broke slowly and ponderously. To the drop in temperature was added the inconvenience of increasingly annoying rainfall. The firing continued spasmodically. When it was properly daylight the police, taking careful precautions, and over a period of two hours, were able to evacuate the tenants living opposite and below them, who'd found themselves trapped. The operation was covered by a fierce round of gunfire from the position overlooking the central well.

The Fire Brigade's largest ladder was propped against the balcony on the second floor, from where the residents could descend, their backs to the street, in the main terrified families who had suffered a situation of extreme anguish for a number of hours. They could observe housewives, their cheeks pale with fear, one of whom was begging that her miniature pooch, a Pekinese, be likewise saved and, together with her owner, placed in a police station, preferably the one on Maldonado Street.

'My daughter and I,' according to Señora Vélez (broadcasting on Radio Carve), 'spent all our time at the far end of the kitchen where, through the plumbing pipes, we heard the lads shouting and guffawing. They're hunting them down like rats . . . It upset me to hear that, you don't kill a Christian like that . . .'

'It seems to me they're all dead,' said Señor Antúnez from the flat next door to number nine. 'It's some time since we heard shouts and guffaws. We're all right, but it was like living through the Second World War.'

Once the adjacent apartments were emptied, the police prepared for the final offensive. Their first move was to order that the running water be cut off, after which came the electricity. Then they employed that super-well-known ruse of a 'Molotov cocktail', mixing them in empty bottles requisitioned from the corner bar. The idea was to throw them into flat number nine, seeking to start a fire that way. Once again, their efforts were in vain, as they were immediately caught and extinguished by the gunmen, who soaked blankets in the bath filled with water and succeeded in putting the fire out without allowing it to spread. Once again and on the spur of the moment, instead of becoming discouraged, the

Argentines redoubled their efforts while the police intensified the gunfire in order to keep them busy.

Whichever way you looked at it, the gunmen's situation had become critical. By taking over flat number three (opposite on the second floor, very close to number nine), the police succeeded in opening up a fresh angle of fire via a skylight, a post occupied by Commissioner Silva and Sergeant Mario Martínez from the Robbery and Larceny Division, the skilled Thompson machine-gun operator. They took it in turns to fire and to reload the weapon. This new breach, which opened a tiny angle with access to the bedroom at number nine, was immediately covered by the bandits.

At eight in the morning, the Argentines resumed shooting their .45 pistols and the machine-guns resumed their response to every round fired by the police. They could only move around in an extremely restricted area of the apartment, as any attempt was blocked by the elite operatives.

At the same time, a special agent from 12a, Aranguren, twenty-one years old, married, and a father of two, together with agent Julio C. Andrada, another youth of twenty-five, were both assigned to the flat, to cover the door giving on to the corridor, a scant three metres away from the gunmen's own front door. One of the malefactors (Dorda) hurled himself into the corridor and, through the half-open door of the adjacent flat, released another burst of machine-gunfire. Aranguren fell where he was and, as they lowered him out of the window and down on to the street, Andrada, a plain-clothes secret policeman, dressed in brown protective clothing, was also wounded and lay where he fell on the kitchen floor of the flat next door, sheltered beneath the sink and far from the reach of the criminals.

Finally, with the building plans in hand, a new method was sought: that of employing members of the fire brigade to perforate the floor of the upstairs flat leading into flat number nine and attack those already under siege from above.

Several policemen climbed up the extending ladder to the second floor where the firefighters had propped it against the window with considerable precision. In order to cover the operation from flat number eleven, a stipple of fire hailed in through the skylights: ditto through the window giving on to the stairwell while the police went into flat number thirteen on the floor above, directly over the besieged den.

That was how, at ten in the morning, a breach was opened in the floor of the flat over that occupied by the Argentines. The idea was to pump carbon monoxide in through the hole, and work was feverishly begun with a steel file in the flat overhead. The task progressed only slowly and in the end a compressor had to be requested from the electricity supply company in order to start working with a power drill.

With the aid of a winch, a pneumatic drill was brought on to the flat roof. They hoisted it up via the corridor on the second floor, which gave on to the roof of one of the bedrooms in flat number nine.

They drilled feverishly and in a few minutes a hole was opened up. The gunmen attempted to stall this latest manoeuvre by firing volley rounds, barely noticing that the hole was now admitting light. The intensity of fire through the windows giving on to the outside stairwells prevented them from gaining positions from which they could aim at their targets with any degree of conviction, let alone hit any of the workmen.

From then on their time was limited. Numerous bottles

filled with petrol were launched through the breach in the ceiling, each with a flaming wick. As it was afterwards confirmed, the floorboards caught fire, all kinds of other objects did too, including furniture and curtains. The air became impossible to breathe.

They were also under direct fire from the breach, from as close as flat number eleven, situated beside that occupied by the gunmen.

Exhausted by the interminable hours of gun battle, having suffered the effects of such a terrible skirmish, the gunmen were once again forced out of the apartment, emerging on to the first floor corridor. At the same time, two cops stationed on the ground floor did the same, coming out into the corridor leading to the staircase, leaving them no option but to hurl themselves towards the front hall of the building, seeking the fresh air of the street. The gunmen crossing the hall without pausing in their shooting got to Miguel Miranda almost on the threshold of the front door, along with another agent with the surname Rocha, who had been posted beside the wall.

From outside there was a rush on the door by the troopers who'd heard another of their number fall, but the wounded cop turned and ran towards the entrance, firing with accuracy, and succeeding in forcing back the gunmen while he dragged Miranda's corpse on to the street.

There was a hubbub of protest and fury from the crowd, and several policemen requested permission to mount a pair of machine-guns, each directed towards the interior of the building, intended to put paid to any further resistance.

Silva's orders, and those of his Uruguayan officers, were to wear down the criminals before coming to the final offensive.

Back inside the flat Dorda and Brignone, like two ghosts, wearing dampened handkerchiefs over their mouths to reduce the effects of the gas, once more abandoned their lair, venturing a couple of metres at a time down the corridor, from where they fired off a number of rounds before again retreating into the apartment.

Their voices floated down from a distance, mingled with muffled sounds, with knocking in the pipes and the interminable barking of a dog. Mereles was leaning up against a door frame beside the kitchen window and now Dorda and Brignone had sat down together, glued to the window overlooking the street.

'How long have we been here?'

Shortly after midday another hefty round of firing resumed, indicating that from first to last the criminals were prepared for anything. Even for death, but only while killing. By now it was assumed that at least one of the gunmen was dead or at least severely injured. The next move was to throw the incendiary bombs into the flat, to succeed in forcing them away from the room with access to the skylight. That gave the further opportunity to other police officers to shoot from a number of different vantage points. That was when the battle climax was reached.

Several men staved in the windows of a neighbouring apartment on the block at number 1182 Julio Herrera, with access on to the street, and gained a foothold there to hold the gunmen at bay by shooting at them from yet another angle, while the drill worked its way through the wall in the adjoining flat. The hole was pushed through at a low level in order that bullets could be used which blazed through surfaces, and which proved more efficacious than those used hitherto.

When the hole was ready the criminals, who never disregarded any possible orifice through which to attack, fired in their turn, wounding another agent from station 12a, Nelson Honorio Gonzálvez, in the chest, causing him to fall immediately from the first-floor balcony to the street below. He was put in an ambulance, but died on the way to hospital.

The police redoubled their offensive and were responded to in kind from inside the apartment, but at the end of half an hour of deafening gunfire, the intensity of fire coming from the gunmen diminished, becoming more and more sporadic. It would seem that they were saving ammunition, but this really wasn't the case, merely that Brignone and Mereles had begun to weaken as a result of the wounds they'd received during fifteen hours of strife.

The only one thus far unhurt was Dorda, who from time to time let off another round of machine-gunfire, in between tending to his two companions. A policeman had been posted outside, in the corridor, and was shooting through the window.

Mereles got up to silence the fire from the sniper posted opposite, but before he could shoot, he received a blast that blew him into the living-room. He had gone into the kitchen to look for an angle of fire and died without being aware of what hit him, as if the effort involved in getting to the light of the window had drawn him beyond the world's domain.

Or so the Kid deduced, as he saw the light shining through the window at the far end, then heard the Crow's groans as he fell on his back against the door into the room.

'Crow,' the Kid said. But the Crow was already dead.

Brignone sat down on the floor, leaning against the wall, firing into the air with his machine-gun, while the police continued their hammering with the pneumatic drill on the roof, making an infernal din as if a train were running overhead.

Mereles had fallen close to the bedroom over which the breach had been opened up. The police barricaded outside behind cars and lorries received the news that possibly one of the criminals was dead. But given the flat's layout, it was impossible either to see inside or to verify the information.

Brignone wanted the Gaucho to fire from the veranda and, holed up in his corner, to give him cover while he went inside the kitchen and fired on to the corridor. They had abandoned the main room where the police were finishing their work on the breach, now opened, beneath the impact of the pneumatic drill that was causing the entire building to judder.

The police threw in a few light hand grenades, but in the end decided to opt for one of maximum potency, dangerous to release, with no guarantee as to where it might land. Commissioner Lincoln Genta slipped it in through the bathroom skylight, connected to flats nine and thirteen. The thing erupted on cue, forcing Brignone to race towards the living-room, where he was hit by the raking of machine-gunfire close to the bathroom door.

He fell flat out in the corridor, face upwards and eyes open, gasping, uncomplaining, extremely pale. The Gaucho was talking to himself in a low voice, in a strange sort of muttering like someone praying, while he dragged himself along the floor, the machine-gun still in his left hand, and approached the Kid.

Finally Dorda came level with the Kid and pulled him up against the wall, out of range, raising him against his body, holding him close, embracing him, half-naked.

They gazed at one another; the Kid was dying. The Blond Gaucho wiped his face and tried not to cry.

'Did I kill the cop who did this to me?' asked the Kid, after a while.

'Of course you did, sweetheart.' Gaucho's voice now sounded calm and loving.

The Kid smiled at him and the Blond Gaucho held him up in his arms like an image of the deposition of Christ. With difficulty, the Kid forced his hand into his shirt pocket and held out a little medal of the Virgin of Luján.

'Don't give in, Marquitos,' said the Kid. He called him by his name for the first time in a long while, in its diminutive form, as if the Gaucho were the one in need of consolation.

Then the Kid raised himself up ever so slightly, leaning on one elbow, and murmured something into his ear which no one could hear, a few words of love, no doubt, uttered under his breath or perhaps left unuttered, but sensed by the Gaucho who kissed the Kid as he departed.

They remained motionless for some moments, the blood coursing between the two of them. Total silence reigned in the apartment. The police leaned down into the breach. They were greeted with a round of machine-gunfire and yells from Dorda, now walled in behind Brignone's body.

'Come on you fat bastards, come up if you dare, let's see what you're made of . . .'

# 9

The afternoon was more or less about to begin, in the midst of the ruined apartment, surprising Gaucho Dorda who found himself suddenly wide awake and sure of himself, his wrap of coke there beside him and something of his life still ahead of him, taken aback by the number of people still in circulation and determined to view this as a good omen.

'When they come to get me, they'll send in one man on his own, perhaps Silva himself, that piece of shit, the ferocious and cowardly Commissioner Silva, he'll come all alone to assassinate me.'

He smiled to himself, lost, immune, propped up against the

door jamb, alert in the damp afternoon light, caressing his machine-gun with his left hand. Ready to die, no way; because nobody's ever ready to die, but prepared to die, yes. Like one endowed with the stigmata, a sign from another age, from whenever, which mark him out: 'You there, you'll come to a bad end.' Encircled, isolated in his lair, enclosed by a ring of death, in the middle of a besieged flat, unable to move, he was prepared to die. The sayings of his dead mother returned like a litany.

'You'll come to a bad end.'

Meaning, dead from a bullet, wounded in the back, betrayed, and none the less he had ended well, whole, without betraying anyone, without allowing his arm to be twisted. He was enthused by his own words and could see, as if in a photo, an arm being twisted, wrestled over the counter in an open-air bar in Cañuelas, followed by his corpse on the front page of the magazine *Crónica*. 'Dorda the hyena is dead.' Let them come, he said, let them come, the rotten bastards. He held out his arm and tied the rubber tube around it, to bring up the vein.

Nothing else mattered. He leant out of the window, to see what the goons were preparing, they were moving around below like little dolls, pinned to the walls, spotlights illuminating the afternoon. At the back, behind them, there was the Rodó Park, and beyond that, the river. Under the ground, below the drains, were the sewers, the giant pipes running like secret passageways and emptying into the river. To escape through the cellars, excavate a tunnel with your hands, get out through those passages via the sewer outlet, climb up the iron staircase, raise the manhole cover and emerge into the fresh air. Some priests ran a school in the midst of the countryside, with trees, estates, and ancient walls.

'Pupil, you'll be enrolled as a pupil.'

And he used to first of all imagine an eye watching over him as he slept, an eye belonging to Pinky Jara, the watchman, blind in one eye, a single eye all white and milky, who beat them all over so that the individual marks couldn't be distinguished. Gaucho used to wet his bed and they made him pick up his mattress and parade before the lot of them, while they laughed at him and he carried his mattress out to dry in the sun, pacing the patio without crying, that Gaucho, until he was sent into the showers, and there, the water streaming all down his face, yes there he could cry without anyone noticing.

'Don't be a pansy, Dorda, don't be a tart, watch out – pansies get pissed on!'

And they laughed, the rest of them, and he threw himself on them, and they all rolled on the ground, hailing blows. 'Pupil', his mother turned him into one to be shot of him, and the word sounded strange to his ears, like a curse. 'You'll attend as a pupil,' his dead mother informed him, and he thought they were talking about an eye operation, making a mark that would forever prevent him from seeing his mother's face, but later, as time went by, he realized it was the girls, whom they'd spy on from the rooftops, through the skylights of the village brothel, getting fucked, their white legs flailing in the air . . . Were they the pupils, were they sending him there? That surely couldn't be so. Madame Iñíguez's pupils, who went for their walks at dawn through the empty village. There were no men in the house on the heights, behind the old corrals, they had to do everything for themselves, the women, with only a handyman to help out, and they got rid of him pretty sharpish, to be all women, living off prostitution, there behind María Juana station. Rusita was the first woman he ever went with, she didn't speak like a Christian, but smiled at him relaying words in a foreign language, all mixed in with a few Argentine words. 'You handsome fellow, pay me a *canario*, come inside me, darling,' uttered with such an air of indifference she might have been totting up bills, or reciting words distantly remembered from a dream. They were on a level, he and the Russian, neither of them really knew how to express their feelings properly. He went to visit and sat down beside her, looking at her as she stroked herself between the legs. For that privilege he paid her what he'd earned or what he'd stolen around the country estates, in the station sidings, in the depths of the store run by Abad, the Turk. They said nothing to one another. The Gaucho was almost speechless during this period of his life, aged fourteen, even thirteen, fair-haired, light-eyed, face flat as a biscuit, and sometimes given to hearing his brainwaves resonate in imaginary tubes like sweet music to the pure and inexplicable voice of Rusita, who spoke to him in her own language, but also called him lovely, handsome and learnt to say My Blond Gaucho and more sweet-talking phrases so incomprehensible that only the two of them could understand, and which entered into the Gaucho through the depths of his heart. He attempted to explain it to her, those roots woven into his heart, belonging to an arbour watered by his blood. And she, what did she understand? He attempted to explain to her. And she knew that he should not be looking for love among women, that his soul could not seek warmth with her kind. He too wanted to tell her things, about the songs his late mother listened to, but his voice wouldn't come out. He practised what he wanted to say to her, but the words tripped him up. Then she looked at him smiling, as if she understood the Gaucho to be different from the rest of them, not effeminate, a true macho, but different from the rest, a pervert they said in the countryside, but not a queer, so, and she buffed her toe-nails, naked, sitting on her bed, the smell of the nail polish remover making him both sick and hot, and he felt like varnishing his own nails, and gazed at the woman with the little balls of cotton wool between her toes, and he wanted to kneel down and kiss her, like the idea of a virgin, but he couldn't manage it and remained there silently, sad, subdued, and from time to time she smiled and spoke to him in her incomprehensible language or sang to him in Polish, the little Russian, and in the end she approached him and the Gaucho permitted his cock to be touched, whether erect or flaccid, without ever succeeding in penetrating her and sometimes it was he who touched Rusita, caressing her as if she were a doll, a little kid he loved in secret, that Blond Gaucho.

This must have all been happening around 1957 or '58. He'd already started going about armed, and she was neither surprised nor afraid, to see him deposit the Ballester Molina on the bedside table, she made as if not to notice, just carrying on, sweetness itself, beneath the night light, speaking her language like a litany. When was that? He can no longer remember. He'd done time twice in borstal, but as yet they'd not sent him to Melchor Romero, as yet they'd not attempted to empty his head with their electric shocks, with their insulin injections, to make him like the rest of them. It was Dr Bunge, with his round spectacles and pointed goatee, who was the first to begin telling him that he had to be made like all the rest. That he had to look for a woman and make a family. Because since forever the Gaucho – who was a killer,

an animal, an assassin, a man quick to anger, feared throughout the province of Santa Fe, and along all the frontier posts –
the Gaucho had always fancied men, agricultural labourers,
old Uruguayan peasants who crossed the river at dawn, from
the far side of María Juana. They took him under the bridges
and sodomized him there (that was the term employed by Dr
Bunge), they sodomized him and obliterated him in a fog of
humiliation and delight, from which he later emerged both
ashamed and liberated. Always detached, always enraged and
unable to say what he felt, with those voices reverberating
inside him, the women who gave him orders and muttered
obscenities to him, issuing contradictory commands, curs-
ing him, and all the voices in Dorda's head belonged to
women. That was why they treated him with injections and
pills in hospital, in order to cure him, to render him deaf to
the voices, to save him from the sin of sodomy. He smiled to
himself now, remembering how he looked at the labourers
with whom he lived during the harvest season. They had to
spend months living closeted together, in high summer, with
the other peasants, and a sunburn that could fry your brains.
Until the afternoon when they were playing at *sapo** together
in the store, all of them pretty much drunk, and they began to
have a go at him, making fun and cracking jokes, and the
Gaucho couldn't respond, he only smiled, with vacant eyes,
and Old Soto took him on, provoking and provoking him
until the Gaucho treacherously killed him, pulled him down
when the old man was attempting to mount his chestnut

---

* It resembles the French *boules*, with a 'toad' instead of a 'pig' that has
to be hit.

mare, and he kept missing his footing in the stirrup and the Gaucho, as if merely wishing to halt this ridiculous dance, took out his weapon and shot him dead.

That was the first dead man in an endless series (or so said the Gaucho, according to Bunge). That was when the epoch of disgrace began and the Gaucho went from being a pick-pocket, a loser, to being an assassin. They took him off to Sierra Chica and put him on bread and water, locking him up until he confessed to what everyone knew. He had clear memories of that period which he recounted to Dr Bunge, who noted every last one of them in his little white note-book.

'If you carry on like this, you'll end up badly, Dorda,' the doctor told him.

'I am already a bad lot,' said the Blond Gaucho, with diffi-culty in expressing himself. 'I've been on the wrong track since I was a child. I'm a hopeless case. I don't know how to express myself, Doctor.'

He waved his hands about to convey what he really felt, but they laughed in his face. He became enraged. 'You'll end up badly,' his late mother went on and on saying to him.

And he'd ended up here. In this flat beside his dead brother, behind a machine-gun aimed at the street, and the street crammed with marksmen out to kill him.

'They'll stake me out, and then they'll send me back to Sierra Chica again, along with the Chileans.' They were hor-rific, the Chileans, they treated him like a beast. 'I'm not going back there. No way will they get me back to Sierra Chica.'

He leaned out of the window, beside the Kid stretched out on the floor of the flat, the medal clasped in his fingers, and the Gaucho could feel him there, dead at his feet, the only man who had ever loved him, and who'd treated him as a person, better than a brother, that Kid Brignone had treated him like a woman, understanding whatever it was he couldn't bring himself to say and so always saying, he the Kid himself, whatever it was the Gaucho felt without being able to express it, as if reading his thoughts. But now he was there, he could see him stretched out with his clear expression, the Kid, covered in blood, face upwards, dead.

He leaned out of the window and looked down on to the street. Downstairs, there was an unusual degree of quiet. He could hear the secret police moving about over his head, as if they were dragging or manoeuvring corrugated iron across the roof.

'Come and get me, bastards,' he yelled. 'I've still got two boxes of bullets.'

He could yell it and could think, without saying as much, 'I've a load of drugs, a wrap of cocaine, enough to stay awake, I've been up that many hours.' Morning had come and then noon, and they were still unable to dislodge them from inside. He stuck his nose into the packet and inhaled, feeling as if it were liberating him, filling his throat like fresh air, a limpid freshness that cleared his head and made him think that he was going to manage to get out of there, to save himself.

He was going to be gone, taking out all the cops he could along with him, they'd sworn as much to one another without actually mentioning it, the Kid Brignone and the Blond Gaucho. On one side of the doorframe they'd made notches with a penknife, there at the entrance, of each cop they'd brought down. There'd been so many it was an effort to remember, around ten or twelve of them. If he'd had a bomb, if he'd had dynamite, he could have tied it to his belt and hurled himself at the street, where all the cops were waiting to watch him die. That way he could be blown to pieces with the lot of them.

Even the crack police were unused to being confronted by men who stood up to them and didn't back down. What they were used to, that useless lot, was to play torturer or hangman, tie you down with bedsprings, shock you until you explode. But when they found someone who stood his ground, who refused to lose his head, they wasted hours in failing to summon up the courage to go and get him.

'Come up and get me, Fatso Silva, you stuck pig.'

To the Gaucho, it was as if his voice came out unwavering, and the entire city listened with rapt attention, his voice resounding like the voice of God from on high, the voice of the Holiest in the Heights, right across the capital. 'Holy Mary Mother of God pray for us sinners now and in the hour of our death Amen.' He recited the prayer on a single exhalation, he recalled every word of the prayer Sister Carmen had taught him. In an orphanage run by nuns who taught him how to pray and sometimes the Gaucho would pray in order to eradicate the voices and he always recited the same prayer to Our Lady the Mother of God.

'Bring me a priest,' he commanded. 'I am going to make my confession.'

They had entered the paved courtyard on horseback and the woman went outside to request they show some respect, with a double-barrelled shotgun under her arm. Where did this memory materialize from?

'I have the right to request a priest. I am a baptized Catholic.'

Shots and some distant voices could be heard from outside.

Now he was calm he knew full well that special branch were there, crawling over the neighbouring apartments. He kept remembering the woman with the shotgun – could it have been his mother? – but then he couldn't remember anything any more, he blanked out, everything vanished into a vacuum, into nothingness. It was the same with his life. The years before the orphanage he could recall perfectly well, thereafter everything was erased, until he met up with the Kid. The days flew by him, and the months never ended. Prison makes the days go by more slowly and the years more quickly. Who said that? From when he came out of prison, he remembered nothing more right up until today, sitting on the floor beside the window, waiting for them to come and kill him.

The Gaucho Dorda had no more voice left to pray. Poor fellow, he was going to die in the Eastern Republic of Uruguay. He had travelled a great deal, his father, who owned a fleet of carts and used them to go harvesting every year, to make money.

A light wind blew in through the inner windows, moving the burnt curtains like ghostly spectres. The Kid's body lay full length on one side of the room, beside the window giving on to the patio. And he could see his father, all of a sudden, who arrived every evening on his skewbald horse.

'What do you have to say, partner . . .'

The horses rapidly became accustomed to the engines of the harvesters, when they came to clear the plantations with the weeds at their height, and they'd rev the accelerator on the regulator, and the horses would pause and, when the problem was dealt with, they'd proceed again. Now images were forming clearly in his mind, of a harvest up in Tandil when he was ten or eleven years old. The speed at which they sewed up the sacks: when the score went up to thirty a hectare, he had to prepare two or three a cart, and in his haste he sewed his shirt tail into one of the sacks. The silk thread in the mouth of the sack needed stitching into a cross, a real cross. He could never learn how to properly sew up the mouths of those sacks. He was semi-retarded, they said, but it wasn't true, he just found it difficult to talk normally, because he was always kept busy arguing with those women muttering things inside his ear. Sewing the words, stitching them to his body, with greasy thread, a tattoo worn on the inside, the words of his dead mother engraved in him as if on a tree trunk.

'They're like flashes of lightning, like thunderclaps, like a white light, memories are,' Dorda announced. 'Here I am, and here I'll stay.'

Everything about him was destroyed, the walls were stripped and broken, bare of plaster, their timbers exposed; a phenomenal quantity of spent lead was scattered through the bedrooms and living-room, the bathroom and the kitchen showed the full force of the fire that had raged there for several hours. What was left at his feet could no longer be recognized as a suite of furniture.

'Come and get me out of here, Silva's merry men, Silva the shit, the pig, let the night reel you in . . .'

On the floor there still lay two .45 pistols, a PAM submachine-gun and a .38 calibre revolver, and in two untidy cases there still remained a few projectiles: that was the arsenal with which the three gunmen had mounted their fifteen-hour-long resistance, under siege from over 300 policemen.

He smiled to himself, sitting alone with his voices reverberating inside him, lower now, then fired off another round, just to let them know he was still there.

They were going to come for him when darkness fell, along the corridors, hunting him down, the search parties. They went around town in a black trap, wearing double-breasted suits. They got down at the station and there they deposited their handcuffed prisoners. They took Crazy Anselmo that way, all the people following behind, they boarded him on to the train, stuck him in an economy class compartment, a cop on either side, because he'd slit the throat of his boss who'd come across him committing a robbery at La Blanqueada. He was an immigrant killer, an assailant, and they'd hunted him through the villages and towns, and found him at dawn in the shunting yard at the station. His boss came down specially to insult him ('Filthy foreign shit') and the old eyetie Anselmo took him out with a stiletto. It was around this time that he, Dorda, must have been how old, maybe twelve or thirteen, around that sort of age, if his memory served him at all. After then nothing, as if someone had come along and erased everything else inside his head, and he'd remained stuck at that period of his life, only able to recall what had happened when he was little and that was it. They took the eyetie Anselmo out of the black trap and stood there waiting for the train to arrive bringing its load of passengers up from the south, on the empty station platform at Pila. The two cops and Crazy Anselmo, in his sandals and grey overalls, because he used to work for the post office, which was where he had started opening the envelopes and stealing their contents, writing letters to the women, then visiting them, and raping them, according to what people said. It seemed as if he only delivered the letters containing bad news, on grounds of his being a superstitious sort. They found the rest of the letters in the basement of his house, clearly logged, and when they found him, he came out shooting, and dedicated himself to rustling cattle and butchering the meat around the province, also to raping country girls in the most remote ranches of its furthest-flung corners. Dorda now managed to remember all of this, leaning out of the window and peering sideways, watching them move, there below in the street.

The killer went with his hands cuffed in front of him, wrists tied to his waistband, but staring haughtily, proud of being an evil man, a rebel, the train tracks staring up at him and the two cops, with their moustaches and ponchos, quietly smoking, because they had the whole line to accompany him down to La Plata, on the passenger train from Bahía Blanca.

'That's how you're going to end up,' the dead woman told him that night.

The skylight in flat three and the breach in the dining-room wall on the second-floor neighbouring flat looking into the bedroom exposed a view of Mereles who had fallen 'dorsally supine' against the bedsprings propped against the far wall. With extreme care one could even perceive, from flat number eleven, Brignone, whose corpse lay in 'an intermediary position' between the kitchen and the hall. Only the third assassin was missing.

The light was now entering between the curtains. He had enough drugs for another couple of hours.

'Bring me some dope,' he yelped.

'Surrender, you piece of shit,' came the reply.

Through the breach opened to next door, the bodies of two gunmen could be seen, lying prone and riddled with innumerable bullets. Poised on the threshold, the foot of one gunman appeared to bear witness to a final attempt at flight in shooting his way out. Then in the flat's dining-cum-living room lay the rest of his bloodstained body, face upwards, submerged in a pool of his own blood that spread out across almost the entire surface of the room. A few centimetres further on lay the other gunman, similarly soaked in his own lake of blood. The first gunman had been dressed in blue jeans and a white shirt; at his side lay his weapon: a Thompson machine-gun. The second gunman had been wearing blue trousers and a brown shirt. The third still remained seated, his back to the window, crouched in an alcove. That man was Dorda.

They ran like rats through the passages, the cops. A priest would come and give him a blessing.

'I'll take one more fix, with your permission, then come and get me if you wish.'

Just in case, they fired off a few more rounds through the breach then chucked more teargas grenades in through the bathroom window. There was no reaction. A policeman leaned out into the corridor and a few seconds later fell riddled by a machine-gun round.

The entrance door to the flat was swinging, like a petrified sign of death, on its lower hinges and bore the traces of a thousand perforations rent by bullets. Trails of splinters and traces of smoke, powder and blood filled the corridor.

He had always been an object of interest for doctors and psychiatrists. The born criminal, the man who had been ruined since boyhood, dying by the law. It was a fate from which there was no escape and to which he had been brought like Anselmo to his economy class carriage in the Southern

Railways. He didn't like the countryside, the plains were boringly flat, but he'd escape during siesta hour and get up on to the harvesters, they had an iron seat, wrought with holes, awkward to clamber on to, and you had to use a plank to brake with. He'd had the good fortune to mount the draught horses which were tethered to the carts, by threading a length of rope through the saddle-rings and under the girth, so the cart could be pulled forward. When you got them up the embankments, you could rest there near the wire fences, choosing the spot for two reasons. Number one, you had a panoramic view of the tracks and secondly because, all along the embankments, you tended to find gopher-holes and you could catch the rodents with the help of the dogs.

He came to the city and went to live in a hostel, down in Barracas, but it was not something he talked about, he hardly even remembered it.

Inside the building, in the alcove where the double bed had been, there was nothing left but a heap of wood shredded by repeated explosions caused by teargas grenades and the raking of machine-gunfire.

The whole place was bathed in blood.

It was as if a demolition company had moved in and completely destroyed the masonry. There was nothing left at all of the building; all that remained standing were the retaining walls.

The police were not inclined to enter. They could not be certain, from the positions they had assumed, whether the three gunmen had committed suicide, or had died by one or another round of machine-gunfire let off against the front door, or else had died by a hand grenade that had been thrown at them from the floor above, through a hole opened up in the roof with a pneumatic drill.

Dorda remained there, his weapons within reach, considering how to shoot his way out to the finale. He had awarded himself one more shot of cocaine.

'Remember, Kid, when you walked down the middle of the road, when you were young, looking for pigeons' eggs in Bolívar, in the summertime. They bathed in the muddy waters of the lagoon and pricked the eggs with a pin and downed the contents in a gulp.'

There was nothing left of the countryside, it was all under surveillance by the cops. He had these fast-flowing images, of a road and a car arriving filled with heavily-armed men. The voices were saying incomprehensible things to him, speaking to him at times in the sweet idiom of the little Polak in the furnished rooms. Who the hell was to know what she wanted to say, or how much she had suffered, poor thing, such a pretty woman, they brought her over by deception, on the pretext of marrying her off to a man of position, but then they locked her up in a boat and brought her into the interior and forced her to work at Madame Iñíguez's establishment (the Chilean woman). She was a peasant girl who knew how to sew and make goulash, and they'd brought her over so she could have a family far from war and hunger. On one occasion he'd decided, as if in a dream, as if it were something he'd heard tell, that the best thing to do would be to kill her, he clearly heard her asking for him to kill her. He didn't want to, he couldn't want to. He tried to get the idea out of his head, but it had taken hold like vermin, like ticks, the voice, and the Gaucho closed his eyes, because the girl was standing at the foot of his bed, naked, with her russet hair reaching to her waist, and he could feel inside his skull a cramp like the wires

transmitting his electric shocks, a voice ordering him to kill
her, addressing him in that idiom peculiar to her that nobody
in the region could comprehend, and yet the words were also
begging him please to do her the favour of saving her, sparing
her from the suffering of being among such brutal peasants
from the neighbouring provinces (yes, exactly that, 'the neighbouring provinces'), nobody understood that she was a Polish
princess who could no longer withstand solitude and suffering ('the suffering'), they had separated her from her daughter,
from Nadia, they had taken her off to a doctor, because they
said she had typhus ('had typhus'). A man gave her 100 pesos
and took the infant wrapped in a napkin, took her off on a
cart, then unloaded her at the brothel in Chivilcoy (as Dorda
explained to Bunge). And the Gaucho understood those
words, the words the Polak was saying, the captured princess,
as though they were agreed signals, and she was telling him
that they had loaded her on to a cart and taken her to the
province of Santa Fe to work with the labourers gathering in
the harvest, to be a camp follower and now she was lost, rel-
egated to a special little cell because the blacks always chose
her, because she was a redhead, a European, but she desired
only to die and she permitted the Gaucho to caress her feet,
and to act as her servant; naked, she stood facing the mirror,
gazing at him with her princess's eyes, begging him to kill her
and the Gaucho paid attention to that voice issuing such
softly-spoken orders, telling him what to do, and reached for
his Beretta down the side of his boot and targeted her eyes and
in that instant her face transformed into an expression of
terror that the Gaucho would never forget, it stayed with him
forever stamped on his brain, the certainty that perhaps she'd
become petrified at the ultimate moment, as happens to sui-

cides when they finally repent and attempt to stay alive after all, and she was entirely nude, her russet hair streaming down her back and her hand raised, like this, in a holy gesture of blessing and terror while the Gaucho blew her head off.

That was how they came to take the psychopath away, killing him with blows and injections strong enough to put horses to sleep, jabs that rendered him a species of zombie, of the living dead, causing all his bones to ache and leaving him unable to rise from his bed for the entire day, this assassin of defenceless women, suffocating in his straitjacket, stuffed into a cell with other madmen raving about wars and lotteries, and him lying there silently listening to his voices and to Rusita's voice begging him to kill her and one evening one of the crazies, Loco Gálvez, appeared with some curved scissors he'd stolen from the sanatorium and liberated all the enraged madmen and let them run off. That was at Christmas 1963, when everyone was preoccupied with the festivities and the Gaucho took a train to Gonnet, got out at Constitución, and began sleeping in the station, which was where he met up with the Kid, who'd recently arrived from Mar del Plata, with a suitcase, after having won a load of loot in the Casino, and whose face seemed familiar to him. They had grown up together in Batán as children, or at least had done time in a borstal there together, and so the Kid brought him along to live with him. He had this mental picture of the Kid coming along the platform, looking amused, with his case, as though he were looking for him, and the Gaucho asleep on a bench against a wall, right at the far end of the platform, when the Kid came up to him and said: 'I know you, you're from Santa Fe. You're the Blond Gaucho, we were in Batán together.'

The Gaucho's memory was functioning none too well, but

when he saw that face in the early morning mist, elegant and joyful as it appeared to him, he was sure it must be true, the Kid looked so like the figure of Christ silhouetted by the station lights.

Commissioner Silva managed to slink his way towards the second floor flat and threw himself in through the ruined door, firing off machine-gun rounds in all directions. The very last gunman, Gaucho Dorda, rose unsteadily to his feet, already 'done in', made a great effort, and fired off his machine-gun without managing to hit his target, he was too weak, and Silva seemed to him to be far too far away, in the clarity of the afternoon light. So he let himself drop, like someone giving in to sleep after a night of insomnia.

With every precaution in place, the police continued their advance, confirming as they did so that two of the gangsters (Mereles 'the Crow' and Brignone 'the Kid') lay dead on the floor, and the third was severely wounded, and on the verge of death.

Shortly afterwards the Chief of Police's call could be heard, signalling towards the street for the firing to cease, given that the criminals were no longer able to offer any further resistance. From the policemen's position could be seen the feet of one of the delinquents, lying by the doorway.

When the journalist, weathered from the battlefields, entered the apartment, the spectacle before him acquired Danteesque dimensions. No other adjective could serve to describe it. Blood flooded the place and it seemed inconceivable that three men could have achieved such decisiveness and heroism. Dorda remained alive, his back against the broken bedhead, embracing the Kid as if he were cradling a toy doll in his arms.

Two paramedics entered and lifted the wounded man, who continued smiling, his eyes wide open and an unintelligible murmur on his lips. When they took Dorda downstairs, curious passers-by and neighbours gathered on the landings, and the cops leapt on him and beat him into unconsciousness. 'A Christ figure,' noted the lad from *El Mundo*, 'the scapegoat, the idiot who has to bear the pain of us all.'

The police were at the point of insurrection when they learnt that one of the gunmen was to be brought out from the building alive. To the cries of 'Murderer' and 'Death to the assassin', they crowded the stretcher and beat the dying man.

When Dorda's bleeding body appeared, its bones clearly broken and, clearly visible, one eye wounded and his belly split open, yet still just alive, it first evoked a response of silence and stupor. The crowds blocked his passage, and the stretcher-bearers were forced to pause.

He was the first to come out, still alive, the first they could see of those evil-doers who had battled heroically for sixteen hours. A fragile body, with the aspect of a boxer, a sacrificial victim, and at the sight of it a wave of loathing flowed through the crowd and when the first man hit him, it was as if the world had caved in, and the dykes of rancour had been breached.

An almost unstoppable avalanche of passion was unleashed on to the luckless man.

Four or five policemen and journalists hit him with their weapons and their cameras, and the wounded gunman became a pool of blood, still living and palpitating, who seemed to continue smiling and murmuring. 'Holy Mary Mother of God, pray for us sinners,' recited the Gaucho. He could see the church and the priest waiting for him in his home parish. Perhaps if he could make his confession, he could obtain atonement, or at least he could explain why he'd killed the redhead, because the voices had told him she no longer wanted to carry on living. In contrast, he himself now wanted to go on living. He wanted to return to lying with the body of the Kid, the two embracing together in bed, in some hostel lost in the remote provinces.

The avalanche encircled him and hundreds of voices rose towards the heavy afternoon sun clamouring for his death.

'Kill him . . . Go on, kill him now! . . . Let him die!'

No one had ever seen anything like it. According to some, the collective renunciation of control was being justified then and there by the terrible and cruel pain caused to society and its laws by the criminals.

The desire for vengeance, which is perhaps the first spark in the electric shock of the human mind when it is cut into, coursed rapidly around the circuit of the crowd. And the crowd heaved: several hundred men and women from all walks of life clamouring for revenge.

The police cordons were by now useless, and the bloody mass that was once Dorda was subjected to a hail of blows from every side, kicks, punches, spitting, insults – every kind of vulgarity and brutality.

Finally he was torn from the tumult, and taken by ambulance to be transferred to the hospital at Maciel. It was 14.15 in the afternoon, and the ambulance into which they'd finally managed to board him was submerged in a human tide.

Then the Argentine Chief of Police spoke, and his voice spread like oil over the troubled waters of the hyper-excited crowd.

He requested calm, he requested pacification in order for

the work of the justice system to take place, he requested a pause for meditation and profound mourning in memory of the departed.

'I've awarded him his last blow,' added Silva.

And over the heads of the crowd, in the heavy air of the afternoon, he raised his right fist, red with blood.

Tears flowed copiously down the round and sagging jowls of Commissioner Silva, mingling with sweat and the afternoon heat, the teargas which still clung lazily to the treetops and the sour scent of blood of two more policemen, dead that very morning on the threshold of the building . . .

Leaving, travelling against the one-way system on Canelones Street and going south, the Public Health ambulance headed towards Maciel Hospital at full speed. 'They haven't killed me, and they're not going to be able to kill me.' He could taste the flavour of blood on his lips and the pain of a smashed tooth and could see the whiteness of the afternoon through his clouded vision.

'My mother always knew that I was destined to be misunderstood and nobody has ever understood me, but occasionally I've succeeded in getting someone to love me. Oh father,' he said as if it were a far-off echo, 'the skewbald horse will come and carry me away from here.' Then at last he could be reunited with the Kid Brignone, in the open country, out in the cornfields, out in the quiet nights. The ambulance siren retreated, and was lost as it turned the corner of the crossroads and Herrera Street was at last empty once more.

# Epilogue

This novel tells a true story. It involves a minor case, already forgotten among police chronicles, which for me none the less, the more I investigated it, acquired the aura and pathos of a legend. The facts occurred in two capital cities (Buenos Aires and Montevideo) between 27 September and 6 November 1965. I have respected the continuity of the action and (wherever possible) the language of the protagonists and the witnesses of this history. Its dialogues and opinions do not in all instances correspond to the precise localities where they were first expressed, but I have always used original material in the account of the words and actions of its characters.

Throughout the book I have attempted to maintain the stylistic register and 'metaphorical gesture' (as Brecht called it) of the social reports whose theme remains illegal violence.

The mass of material documentation has been deployed as dictated by the plot, meaning that whenever I have been unable to confirm the facts with direct sources, I have opted to omit that particular version. This explains why the great unknown of the book (its 'fantastical instant') has to be the mysterious disappearance of Enrique Mario Malito, the gang's leader. Nobody really knows what happened to him in the hours following the siege. Numerous hypotheses exist regarding his fate but I have chosen to respect the intrigue woven by the story's protagonists.

Some say he split from the gang at the moment when they were surprised changing the plates on the Studebaker and that he travelled in the Hillman to get away from Marmajará Street ahead of the confrontation with the police. He had a rendezvous arranged with Brignone for the next day, but the succession of captures and the siege of the block of flats cut their connection. The most plausible account assures us that, despite being isolated and without contacts, he managed to escape and cross to Buenos Aires and that he died in a shoot-out in Floresta in 1969. The most extravagant version recounts that he managed to flee over the rooftops just as the police arrived, and that he hid himself in a water tank where he remained alive for two days until he could escape to Paraguay where he lived in Asunción until his death (from cancer) in 1982 under an assumed name (that of Aníbal Stocker, according to some sources).

For his part, the Gaucho Dorda recovered from his wounds and was extradited to Buenos Aires where he died the following year, assassinated during a revolt that took place in Caseros jail (it would appear to have been initiated by a police infiltrator). During his stay in hospital and in prison (in Uruguay) in January and February of 1966, he was interviewed by the employee of the daily *El Mundo* from Buenos Aires, which published some of Dorda's statements in features published on 14 and 15 March 1966. In addition, I obtained access to the transcripts of Dorda's interrogation, which reside in the annals of the case and the psychiatric reports of Dr Amadeo Bunge. I owe a further debt of gratitude to my friend Dr Aníbal Reynal, a judge of the primary courts, for granting me permission to consult and index this mass of material. The assistance of the judge of Assizes of the 12th District of Montevideo, Dr Nelson Sassia, was of immense value, for he allowed me to work with the statements of witnesses and the clerks to the court used in the case. It was here I came across the testimonial accounts offered by Margarita Taibo, Nando Heguilein and Yamandú Raymond Acevedo, among others of those involved. In Buenos Aires, the lawyer Raúl Anaya permitted me to consult records of the interrogations of Blanca Galeano, Fontán Reyes, Carlos Nino and others implicated in the case. I also obtained access to the declarations of Police Commissioner Cayetano Silva in his internal summary when he was obliged to bring a defence in an internal inquiry mounted by the police on grounds of his presumed complicity (an investigation that reached no final conclusion on the matter).

The remaining significant source for this book was the transcript of the secret recordings made by the police department on Herrera and Obes Streets, to which I obtained access thanks to an order of Dr Sassia, who facilitated my work with this confidential material. In November 1965 the Montevideo newspaper *Marcha* published a lengthy interview done by journalist Carlos M. Gutiérrez with the Uruguayan radio operator Roque Pérez, responsible for the technical control of all the recordings made in the apartment block at the time.

Naturally, I also went to the archives of all the newspapers published during that period. In Buenos Aires there were the *Crónica, Clarín, La Nación* and *La Razón de Buenos Aires;* in Montevideo, *El Día, Acción, El País* and *Debate.* Of particular usefulness were the accounts and additional notes signed simply E.R., who covered the assault and served as the Argentine paper *El Mundo*'s special reporter on the spot. I have freely reproduced from these accounts, without which it would have been impossible to obtain an exact reconstruction of the facts narrated in this book.

Thanks to the generosity of my friend the sculptor Carlos Boccardo, who lived in Montevideo throughout the events described on the corner of Herrera and Obes Streets, I was able to orchestrate the different versions of this same story from a variety of descriptions and evidence.

My first link to the story as related in this book (as always happens in every non-fictional account) occurred by chance. One afternoon, at the end of March or beginning of April 1966, I took a train *en route* to Bolivia. There I met Blanca Galeano, called by the newspapers 'the concubine' of the gunman Mereles ('the Crow'). She was sixteen years old but looked like a woman of thirty, and was in the process of flee-ing the authorities. She told me an extraordinary tale which I half-believed, tailoring it to elicit (as indeed it did) a quantity of meals taken in the train's buffet car. During the long hours of the journey, which lasted over two days, she told me that she had just been released from jail; that she had been held a prisoner for six months for associating with a gang of thieves who had robbed the San Fernando Bank; and that she was going into exile to live in the Bolivian capital of La Paz. She gave me a first, muddled version of the deeds I vaguely recalled having read in the dailies some months earlier.

The girl spoke of a gangster who had taught her about the other side of life, and who had since died, brought down after having resisted like a hero for fifteen hours, and sparked in me the initial interest in her story. 'There were around three hundred cops, and they held out surrounded by the lot of them, but nobody could smoke them out of their lair,' the girl said in a vocabulary that sounded hostile, like words angrily used to describe a defeat that should have ended in victory. The kid had given up attending secondary school, become a cocaine junkie (as I could confirm after only a short time travelling together), though she described herself as the daughter of a judge, and swore that the Crow had left her pregnant. She spoke to me about the Twins, Kid Brignone and Gaucho Dorda, and about Malito and Twisty Bazán, and I listened to her as if brought face to face with the Argentine version of a Greek tragedy. The heroes were determined to confront and resist the insurmountable, and chose death as their destiny.

I got out in San Salvador, in Jujuy province, because I wanted to reach Yaví for the Holy Week processions. The train stopped for half an hour for the railway gauges to be changed. She got out with me, and we bade one another farewell at the zinc counter of a bar alongside the platform, where we drank a Brazilian beer together. I recall taking notes of what she told me both on the train and at the station, then again when I reached the hotel (for in those days I still considered that a writer had to go everywhere with his journalist's notepad). Then a while later (in 1968 or '69) I started properly researching the story, and wrote a first draft of this book.

It will always remain a mystery to me why the motives for recounting particular stories lie dormant for years on end, awaiting the proper moment to make their mark. I left off the project in 1970 and stored the drafts and the supporting material at my brother's home. Some time later, in the midst of moving house, I came across the box containing the manuscripts and documents, including the first results of my research and the first version of my book. In the summer of 1995, I began writing it all over again, giving it a complete overhaul in order to be absolutely faithful to the facts. The events it recounted were now so distant and hermetically closed that they resembled the lost memories of a lived experience. I had almost forgotten what they were, so much so they appeared new and nearly unknown to me, after a period of more than thirty years. This distance has helped me to work with the story as if it were the account of a dream.

It seems to me that this dream opens with an image. I would like to end this book with the memory of this image, meaning the memory of the young girl travelling on the train to Bolivia, leaning out of the window with a serious expression on her face, tranquil and without any parting gesture, while I, standing on the empty station platform, watch her recede into the distance.

*Buenos Aires, 25 July 1997*